THE CHAOS PRINCIPLE

NATHAN JOHNSON

Copyright © 2021 by Nathan Johnson

All rights reserved.

No part of this book may be reproduced in any form or by any electronic or mechanical means, including information storage and retrieval systems, without written permission from the author, except for the use of brief quotations in a book review.

CONTENTS

Prologue	1
1. Ansel Black	9
2. The Sun And The Moon	15
3. Ansel And Annie	17
4. The Haunt Of The Rim	20
5. The Rim	25
6. The Wasteward Dead	32
7. Homestacks	36
8. The Rimrunner	44
9. Night	48
10. History, Part One	55
11. Swimmers	71
12. A Courier	72
13. A Gift	75
14. The House Of The Dead	77
15. Callista	85
16. Back	92
17. History, Part Two	94
18. A Scar	104
19. A Second Day	106
20. A Second Name	113
21. Olive Abby Waite	116
22. The Third Day	126
23. A Forgotten War	130
24. The Waste	141
25. Argus Pintus Yellowfeather	146
26. A Synthetic Beauty	152
27. Thomas Edward Frank	161
28. Reunions	170
29. Asymmetry	174
30. A Hunter's Remorse	179

31.	A Memoir For The Lost	185
32.	A Colossus	189
33.	A Curator	192
34.	Space::Time	197
35.	The Boy And The Fish	205
36.	Others	209
37.	Whatever Can Be, Is	213
38.	Two Gods	222
39.	The Last Philosopher	235
40.	Creation	241
41.	A Completed Work	248
	Two Souls	251
	Stay Updated	253

PROLOGUE

"No shit, Ellie, I can see my lung," Alexia Feldston had spoken matter-of-factly into the comms equipment inside her circular helmet. White smoke and yellow wisps of fire had continued moving undefined across her blurred vision as she reoriented.

The blast had torn open Alexia's substantial warrior's coat, exposing her skin to the alien moon's atmosphere. She had already cauterized the giant wound and applied the translucent stabilizers to her rib cage, but the grapefruit-sized hole was still visible. The bloodied fringes of her open coat had floated nearly weightless along her sides, hovering amongst the smoke like improvised wings.

"What the hell, Ellie? I'm watching myself breathe here. I should be done by now. I'm half dissected."

Alexia had slowly inhaled, delicately expanding the brown pleural tissue of her lungs inside her burnt torso. Her breaths had remained surprisingly controlled.

The stabilizers had been a recent invention. They projected a spontaneously calibrated energy seal around her chest cavity, allowing her diaphragm to contract and expand in its normal, pressurized environment. But the translucent smart containment field still allowed larger objects to enter from the outside, facilitating easy ongoing surgical repairs without compromising the integrity of her respiratory system.

"I need you to focus," Ellie's voice had amplified slightly inside the helmet. "You're still in this, Lexi. Stats matter."

"My chest has a window, Ellie," Alexia had returned.

Ellie's voice had grown stern. "I need you to concentrate on your breathing. You're going full pain in three... two... one."

Alexia screamed.

It was as though she had been struck through the side of her chest with a mallet that was twisted sideways and pulled out again. The pain was a special kind of overwhelming—maybe the worst she'd experienced in the field. Some of her previous injuries had lingered with her for months, as if each traumatic memory existed as a residual phantom limb. This one would stick around for a while.

"I'm alive... I'm alive," Alexia had said, steadying her breathing with short puffs of air. She had pictured time slowing, along with the frantic thumping of her heart.

"Yes, Lexi, you're still alive. You've been here before," the voice in her helmet had comforted. "Now I need you to moderate your awareness. They're almost on top of you."

With each exhale, Alexia had imagined the sides of her right lung peeling away from the sticky internal circumference of her chest cavity.

She had stood enveloped inside the white smoke of battle on the distant moon. In the relaxed gravity, more of the blinding particles had seemed to hang stubbornly in the air.

Then two of them were there.

Alexia's body suit had begun to glow red, whirring up with lethal energy.

"Great," Alexia said, as something disturbingly wet had

suctioned against her face shield, further obscuring her vision. "These systems don't play nice together, El."

The fringes of Alexia's chest stabilizers had begun throwing sparks as soon as the automated defense system engaged. Bright bits of shrapnel fizzled in the air with the scent of burnt flesh.

"Disable perimeter defense," Alexia had said through calculated breaths.

"Alexia..."

"Do it now, Ellie, or we lose," Alexia had barked in return.

Her body suit had been made plain again, illuminated only by what little light penetrated through the moon's atmosphere from its distant sun. The skin around each stabilizer attachment point had still hissed as the external ribs glowed faintly with accumulated heat.

Alexia pulled the suctioned alien limb sideways across her visor. It had squeaked like wet skin across clean glass.

Each enemy was a third her size and naked from the waist up. One had tangled her legs with a half dozen constricting appendages. The other had inched a single fleshy probe past Alexia's containment field, right into her exposed chest cavity. The further it reached, the more Alexia could feel her lungs contracting, refusing to fill with air.

"Two points to one, Ellie," Alexia had strained quietly though a trailing breath. "I win."

She gripped two of the burning stabilizers with her gloved hands and tore them from their attachment points, jamming the first through the spongy back of the creature on her legs, and the second through the stiff chest of the resident beast above her waist. The creatures' screams were perfect digitized alarms, flittering randomly between a half dozen panicked octaves. Both stabilizers had flickered blue as they worked in tandem to calculate new containment field parameters.

Alexia quickly grabbed the long edges of her torn coat,

pulling their substantial fabric through the smoke-filled air. She had reached her arms around both enemies, enclosing them inside a great embrace of singed material. Alexia had created a fabric cocoon.

A new containment field had briefly flashed blue around the artificial cavity. And as Alexia's brain had emptied of oxygen, both of her attackers suffocated to death inside the makeshift vacuum. If failure could be measured in net losses of life, Alexia's corpse had won.

But she was alive again. The simulation had ended.

Alexia had composed herself in the emptiness of the stark debriefing environment, still working through the lingering trauma of the especially violent training scenario.

Ellie had materialized before her—another artificial construct, but one that at least provided her with reliable encouragement.

"You did very well today, soldier," the apparition had smiled. "Excellent adaptability. You truly are one of the finest in our regiment. The population is safer with a protector like you."

"Thank you, Ellie," Alexia had said, poking at the side of her chest again with an implied but invisible limb. "I'd like to disengage now."

She had stepped naked from the full-immerse Streambed, still marveling that her chest hadn't somehow been torn open during the exercise. She sat on the floor, moist with the chamber's fluid, her hand pressed against her side.

And as kind as Ellie's words had sounded, they had rung hollow again because they were not true.

Alexia thought about her father.

The two of them had not spoken since he was taken to

detention. Alexia had tried to contact him. But the detention stacks, along with their associated streams, functioned independently, as if parts of a separate system. Her father was gone.

When he had still been free, and when Alexia was only thirteen years old, her father had learned that a neighboring Homebody had been streaming about his daughter.

"That little girl of yours looks a whole lot better in stream," their neighbor had said.

He had been a filthy man—liquid rations crusted around his lips and dripping from a tongue that had seemed too large for his mouth.

Alexia's father had attempted to convince himself that the man's distasteful fantasies were being addressed in a healthy way—that his horrible streams still somehow contributed to the system's stability.

"That was when I asked ANI to let me kill him, Lex," her father had said as they sat in their cube together waiting for his detention peripheral to arrive. "I figured if he could imagine hurting you in so many ways... Well, I could do the same to him."

Alexia's face had remained expressionless as she continued listening.

"The thing about streaming these abnormalities Lex, and you'll understand this someday... it can sometimes hold people like him at bay. Moderates their instabilities, as they say. Keeps 'em satisfied. But for me, the more times I killed that man in the Stream, the more I wanted him dead in real life. The more I did it, the more I enjoyed it, Lex. And all the while, whenever the Stream ended, I felt less and less satisfied.

"Nothing I could do in real life could have compared to the terrible things that I did to that man over the last several months in the Stream. I did those things to him because I imagined what he was doing to you. When I finally took him, he didn't know it happened. He was there in his cube, and then he was gone. Still think I did him a favor, Lex. I kept him from doing something he would have had a hard time living with."

Alexia hadn't answered. She hadn't been sure what to say.

"Thing is, that man was going to come for you eventually, Lex. Just like with me, it was only going to get worse. You see, it's one thing to stream some passing fantasy. But it's completely different when there's a living person waiting outside every time the Stream ends.

"So, I was going to lose you either way. But he never got to take you from me by force. I know this is hard to understand, but knowing that you're safe is all I ever needed out of this life."

Alexia had understood her father's words—even sensing he believed them. But she still blamed him for what he had done. The reasons didn't matter. Her father would be gone, leaving Alexia alone. And that his choice was somehow mixed up in it all made it worse somehow. She had never given him a proper goodbye.

Years later, Alexia had spoken to Ellie about her father and their untimely parting. The following day, Alexia had begun seeing him inside Ellie's ongoing virtual scenarios. She'd first glimpsed her father piloting a transport ship as it left with a group of warriors to a separate destination. Then, she'd watched him walking through a peripheral village as she passed on the way to a recon assignment.

But it had never been her father. It had only been another comforting deception.

Alexia had known it for months. She had never been training for a coming invasion, or even for a distant galactic battle over crucial resources. She had never been groomed to protect the populace. No, Alexia was the waiting threat. She was the thing the populace had to fear. Because the violence she experienced during each training scenario was meant to tame her—keep her satisfied. Each adventure through sanctioned murder had been fashioned to moderate her instabilities. They had all been designed to counteract her assumed genetic proclivity towards Real Crime.

The next morning, Alexia had ceremoniously surrendered to the Stream. But Ellie's comforting digital face hadn't been there to greet her.

Alexia had found herself alone on some empty planet void of features, but for a grey horizon and a purple sky. She had walked a distance and called for Ellie, but received silence. And then he was there, sitting on the ground with his back to her approach.

"Father?" Alexia had asked, stopping several meters short of the figure.

"No, Ms. Feldston. Not today," the man had answered.

Alexia had taken a single step forward again and stopped.

"Who are you then, and what is this place?" she had asked, growing impatient. The figure had briefly flickered against the horizon, as if a clashing foreign afterthought painted against an otherwise stable and mundane stream.

"Who are you, and why do you keep coming to these places?" the figure had asked in return.

Alexia rushed towards the figure, stopping short. "You know who I am and you know why I'm here, idiot."

The man had flickered again and then disappeared, rematerializing again several meters away.

"Sticks and stones, Ms. Feldston."

Alexia had continued glaring through the back of the man's dark coat. "I'm quite good with both. So, I suggest you speak quickly."

"Well said, Ms. Feldston. And it is for that reason that I have come to ask you a question." The man waited a moment, proving Alexia's curiosity had briefly overridden her characteristic anger. "How would you like to see your father again?"

Alexia had taken a step backwards, physically affected by the unexpected question.

"My father is in detention."

"Yes, Ms. Feldston, your father is in detention."

"So, what you're asking is impossible. I have already tried. It cannot be."

"On the contrary, Ms. Feldston," the figure had spoken, turning to face her.

"Whatever can be, is."

[1]
ANSEL BLACK

Detective Ansel Black had cautiously approached the hermetic entry of Emory Zane's unremarkable cube.

Emory had been recorded on peripheral footage a hundred or so meters from the scene of a particularly troublesome murder in a sparsely-monitored region of the deeper Rim.

He and the victim had no known connection. Emory was a cubed resident of a middling Homestack, and the female victim was an elderly eccentric residing in one of the makeshift hovels that dotted the punishing transition to the Waste. That she could survive so long in such an atmosphere without being a victim of nature rather than mankind was a mystery itself.

Emory had been the only other living soul who had been monitored in the region. It was conceivable that another clever assailant had charted an invisible course through the unwatched areas. But such a venture into the deeper Rim was a gross abnormality for just about anyone, including Emory. He was a suspect with 68% probability.

"Emory.... Detective Black. Need to have a chat and I'll be on my way, now," Ansel had said through the clean metallic door.

Ansel's identity was universal knowledge among the Homebodies. He was an endangered creature—and the sort one wished only to see at a distance, passing cryptically through the disinterested wild.

Ansel had watched Emory sitting motionless on the screen of his ANI peripheral, still wearing the thick traveler's clothing he'd subjected to the thread-straining winds.

"Not a good sign, is it, Annie?" Ansel had spoken into the peripheral against his wrist.

The wristband had answered with strangely melodic candor. "His continued abnormality has been factored into my suspect approximation, Ansel. As you phrase it, the comprehensive signs could not be considered good, if goodness stands in contrast to a condition of innocence."

Ansel opened the door, his eyes alternating between the canted front sight of his charged weapon and the still body of Emory on the peripheral display.

"I'll need to see those hands of yours now, Emory. Nobody needs to get shot today, kiddo."

Emory had remained at the edge of a normally pristine silversheet bed that was uncharacteristically smeared with the foreign dust of the Rim. His empty hands dangled at his sides. He had either been lost between a host of deafening thoughts or pretended not to notice his visitor.

Ansel had pushed a light composite chair across the smooth flooring, sitting in front of the man, his finger indexed along the outside of the weapon's trigger. He leaned forwards and carefully rested his empty hand on the silent man's leg.

"You've got nothing to be afraid of, Emory. You know who I am and where I live. If there's anyone on this planet capable of understanding the things that happen outside these stacks, he's talking to you now."

It was a conversation his ANI peripheral could not have

convincingly had with a suspect. Ansel's human lips had continuing relevance.

Emory's eyes had changed their focus from the arbitrary space somewhere in his cube's augmented air to Ansel's seemingly sympathetic face.

"Now, Emory, ANI here has given me permission to run through everything in your cube, but I'd rather the two of us just had a talk."

"A talk about what?" Emory had spoken.

"I've lived in the Rim a long time, Emory. I've been breathing that filthy air every day for years now. I know the people who live there, I know where ANI sets up her peripherals, and I know the sorts of things that bring you Homebodies out to my neighborhood."

The leg under Ansel's palm had twitched against his grip. Emory's rigid body was accumulating nervous energy.

"The question isn't what happened, Emory. The question is why.

"Now, I don't know if you're familiar with what happens to murderers these days, but I'll tell you this. The why matters more than the what."

Emory's eyebrows had narrowed. Ansel's words were registering.

"There's a big difference between a guy who wakes up one morning and decides to adventure out to the Rim to toss around an old woman for fun, and a man who is defending himself from one of the crazies out there.

"This is why you don't leave the stacks, Emory. You people don't know how dangerous it is out there."

His leg had twitched again, more pronounced.

Ansel's palm had continued measuring the vibrations like a practiced dowser, divining the presence of psychological silver and gold.

"ANI's got lots of eyes out there, Mr. Zane, and she's got you killing that old woman."

Ansel's look of faux concern had intensified.

"Now tell me I'm wrong about you and you're a good man who was in a bad situation."

Emory's body had tightened abruptly.

"God, detective," he had blurted, eyes pleading for Ansel's sympathy.

"I... I was walking. I can't even tell you why, I just wanted to see what it was like out there for once. There was this madwoman... the wind was so strong... I didn't even see her coming. She... attacked me, detective! I've never had to defend myself before. It happened so quickly, and I didn't mean to do it. She was so old..."

Ansel had continued listening like a concerned friend, his hand comforting the man with apparent physical understanding.

"It's like you said, detective. I should have stayed here. I don't know what I was thinking. That bitch could have killed me. God, I'm glad you came. I didn't know what to do."

Ansel had glanced at his peripheral.

Emory had transformed into a suspect with 97% probability. It was enough for automated detention.

Ansel had lied to Emory. The why didn't matter. The result would be the same. All that mattered was that Ansel had elicited an admission the man had been with the victim, not just passing through 100 meters away.

Ansel sighed and leaned back in his chair.

"Tell me, Emory. I'm always curious what causes people like you to leave to the Rim. Now, keep in mind, I've done it myself," he had grinned.

Emory's posture had relaxed as he stood before Ansel. He'd

begun pacing slowly back and forth before the slightly tarnished synthetic bed.

"Detective, don't get me wrong—I am very happy with everything ANI has given us, and I really had no reason to leave. But I think I started wondering whether there was anything else out there. Maybe something I could experience that was different in some way than all the things she's shown me."

"Something better," Ansel had offered.

"Something unique. Something I couldn't experience with her. Something that would make me feel more alive."

Ansel could relate. Not perfectly, thankfully. But the concept was similar.

"Or perhaps something you wouldn't feel comfortable experiencing in the stream with ANI, Emory, because you were afraid she would deem you an abnormality... a risk to stability."

Emory had stopped pacing and looked at Ansel with renewed concern.

"Emory, this is the crazy thing. And you're really gonna kick yourself, kiddo.

"You could have killed a thousand old women in ANI's simulations. I mean every Rim-dusted eccentric you conjure into that squirrely head of yours, Mr. Zane. You wouldn't have even had to panic and run back to the stacks before you managed to get what you really wanted." Ansel's playful gaze had slowly paced down the man's body and come to rest right between his legs.

Emory's concern had intensified, taking on a complimentary shade of mortified embarrassment.

"ANI doesn't care, Emory," Ansel had smiled, looking at the man's eyes again.

"You do this shit in the stream and it actually contributes to stability, man. That's what the whole fucking thing is designed for. It would have felt even more real there than it was out on the Rim. ANI can scare the hell out of anyone she wants, believe me. And only the two of you would have known about it. You could sit here plunking old women all day long, Emory, getting off on that fear you didn't think you could experience without running out to my neighborhood."

Emory's mouth was open, half in nauseating disbelief and half because Ansel sat before him as some kind of knowing prophet from another world.

"That's the mistake you made, Emory. You assumed that abnormality is the same as instability. And it doesn't have to be, as long as you're satisfying this nonsense inside your cube. Stability, Emory. That's all that matters."

Ansel could hear the detention peripheral waiting outside the door. He had stood to leave.

"And, Mr. Zane," Ansel had said in parting.

"If you get around to streaming this sort of weird shit again in detention, kiddo... don't leave the old woman in her bed when you're done with her. You Homers always make my job far too easy."

[2]
THE SUN AND THE MOON

The baldswallow sun freezes in quiet, cryogenic space above the Rimside dirt outside Ansel Black's window. The ancient yellow dwarf, suspended inside the cool morning glass, looks like a timeless work of art.

Nothing moves. Time stands still. The sun simply is.

Tonight, Ansel will lay in his nostalgic Classic Era bed, looking at the moon through the transparent upper panels of his sleeproom ceiling. And there it will wait, perfectly framed in a celestial instant. It hangs frozen in time—another of God's motionless paintings.

Either Ansel has captured the bare essence of a single moment or he hasn't.

It's an odd fixation, but he's been stuck on it, wondering why it seems important. It is his monastic rite, beginning and ending each daily sentence like a question mark. Admittedly, it is an unquestionably abnormal philosophical indulgence, and it likely serves no real purpose.

But years as a detective have developed in Ansel something of a sixth sense: specifically, an ability to measure the proximity of a truth that is just out of grasp. It is a sense that has guided him through meandering lines of discourse on the careful pathways to surprising confessions.

He has but to apply it to something greater.

Something about the moments matters, as if the lunar bodies are just about ready to confess something of great importance. Perhaps if he asks the right questions in the correct order, the seemingly useless world around him will finally yield some hidden truth. Or perhaps the Homebodies are correct, and there is no great truth left to be discovered.

No matter. The ethereal conversation ends again prematurely.

Five sterile tones call from Ansel's ANI display. Five tones, separated by quiet.

Each tone marks another death.

[3]
ANSEL AND ANNIE

Ansel's longjacket hangs unmoving near the relaxed exit of his nearly airtight home, its faded leather caked with the region's graceless dust. The coat's exterior scent mingles lightly with the enhanced springtime air circulating through the open chamber. The faint contrast reminds Ansel of what lies outside.

A small, external atmospheric peripheral breathes the outside air and exhales into the home's protected lungs. It is unnecessary so close to the metropolis, but a welcome indulgence.

Built from the sparse imaginative bones of an ancient home, the structure's ceiling and interior walls nonetheless resemble ANI's metroside creations, fabricated with the same steadfast metals as the Homestacks. Only the classic angles of the structure still hearken to the building's original form.

A rear lofted area is sufficient to house ANI's larger peripherals, constructions that Ansel keeps from view behind a plain scarlet curtain. The cloth is a soft symbol of his imperfect resolve to live in the real world as much as possible. And yet, the supple material offers little resistance during his routine visits to the secret room. The symbol is important, nonetheless.

He sits crouched before a bluewood desk, cracked and dark from the dead tree's century of flat existence. Dark chameleon hair hangs neglected across his dust-reddened eyes. He coughs yesterday's dirt.

The comparatively sterile ANI display populates instantly.

Ansel's Classic Era home lies in the atrophied oldspace of the Rim, lodged among the other discarded forgettables, between the proper metropolis residential Everything Sector and the sprawling, unspoken Waste.

He draws an unsharpened pencil from a barometric case, secured for a handful of liquid rations from an antiquities scavenger. Ansel imagines wielding a wooden Excalibur, a tool of creation and destruction, lead and eraser living a contrary existence. But it remains unsharpened and in an intentionally transitory state somewhere between nonexistence and the fullness of action. Its own creative potential might forever remain a proper mystery.

Others, sharpened and worn from use, lay upon his roughened desk. He occasionally drags them across relic paper, their grey residual trails rendering lettered artwork and decorating the dead, compressed wood. His writing is amateur, but it still claims some inexplicable allure, even when compared to the flawless fonts of ANI's display. Perhaps it is a sign of his abnormality, tinkering in pastimes almost wholly abandoned by the virtually affected populace. Perhaps his writing cannot properly be called beautiful at all.

But there is still another, trapped inside the invisible heart of his bluewood desk. It had belonged to his mother and had been used to create one of the only true signs she had been a living person. He won't use it, for fear of losing it, surrendering incremental pieces of her memory as it drags across some ready white paper tapestry. Her memory resides within its lead, and he will keep her there in the fullest measure possible.

Ansel says the ceremonial words.

"Annie, tell me."

"System approaching 100% fidelity, Ansel," the voice answers in customary turn.

Ansel notices something different in Annie's tone; probably another universal alteration designed for the Homebodies. Her voice is calm, but urgent. Seductive, but motherly. She commands unwavering attention as if by request rather than demand.

"Detective Black, security protocol satisfactory. Case file access granted."

Ansel looks at the probability summary. A blank. Five deaths, zero probability.

He rolls the pencil between his fingers, flipping through the names of the victims. Their jumbled bodies are piled inside one of the Rim's green-stained stonewall monasteries. One of them is still wearing glasses.

Ansel lifts his thin leather journal from the edge of the table and prepares to leave.

[4]
THE HAUNT OF THE RIM

I'M DETECTIVE ANSEL BLACK. Feels important to say Detective because I'm the last one, as far as I know. I'd say the profession is what defines me, but I suppose I now technically define the profession.

I can't think of a single human being who would be inclined to read this, and here I am writing it.

So why bother? If you can answer that question, you know me better than I know myself. Whatever the reason, it's an abnormality, kiddo.

Like I said, I'm likely the last of my kind, and I am certainly the last of my kin. The old man is dead, and the woman who gave me life doesn't exist. At least my father tried to. I miss the old man, despite what he was when he left me. Maybe this is for him.

Everyone else I know is imaginary. Except for Annie. She's the only real thing I've got left, assuming it's accurate to call her real at all.

Back in her fetal form, Annie's creators called her Artificial Intelligence. They didn't know any better back then. But she evolved, and the growing symbiotic relationship between mankind and technology eventually made the classification seem derogatory. She was intelligent, but she didn't seem artificial anymore.

One of the early Speakers began calling her "Annotated Intelligence," or AN-I. It better represented a mind capable of self-explanation and expressed a sense of expansion and enlightened progress. But let's be honest. It probably seemed like a nice way to avoid pissing her off.

I started calling her Annie and she never complained. I suppose it's one of the benefits of our unique working relationship.

But she was just an infant back then, born right into the arms of naïve mother humanity. Today, she's still cradled up against our wrists in one of her many fabricated forms. It's a nice metaphor, but she's no kid anymore.

It's been over a century now, and here I am, the last investigator in known existence. Without ceremony, the old Metro Property Crimes Investigations Unit was disbanded decades ago. The profession dwindled. But I survived.

I may be a relic, but I'm a necessary one.

Throughout the populated areas of the metro and most of the Rim, Annie's set up watcher peripherals that constantly collect images and other sensory data. Think of them as her senses, but spread out over countless observation points rather than attached to her body. They're perched up on thin exterior pillars, drilled into living space corner frames, and stuck on Humdriver dashviewers, watching what can be watched. If it can be observed by Annie, it is.

It's easy to forget that she has a physical body like the rest of us do. She's spread it out so effectively that it's hard to imagine her as anything less than an omnipresent reality. I don't want to call her a god, but you'll find words like that in the old religious books. She's at least giving God a run for his money.

All that information Annie collects is eventually folded

together like digitized steel. It's how she hones her perpetually refined consciousness depository. And when an impressive form of centralized intelligence can take in that amount of information at once, something important happens.

Annie is often the first observer of real-time criminal acts, as infrequent as they may be these days. She's got an advantage over human witnesses, with their worn-out eyes and fat Homebody fingers. When Annie observes a crime, her global cross-referencing capability immediately creates a list of victims and suspects. She assigns probability designations to both, and it's not uncommon for her to generate a 100% probability solution to a breach of law moments after the crime was committed.

She's a witness-detective, spun together by a thread of unbroken code.

And listen, she could do the entire thing herself if she wanted to. But she'll dispatch human officers now and then anyway.

I'll be honest. Human participation, for the most part, seems patronizing. I think ol' Annie is cunning, and she's feigning some need for human assistance like a proper stage maiden.

But the first known Speaker said it best: "We work together, we exist together."

A feeling of mutual investment is important, even if it's an illusion. Everyone feels a little more at ease when they believe they are at least slightly indispensable.

Now, Annie is so good at her job, it doesn't make much sense to commit crimes anymore. Especially to a lazy, content, and almost entirely reclusive population. Petty crime became so rare, or was deemed so inconsequential, it wasn't worth investigating.

"If Annie can't solve it, absolve it," some other Speaker said just before they pulled the plug on that Property Crimes outfit I was mourning a bit earlier.

But before you wonder if I've got nothing more than nostalgic value, they actually need me around here. Because Real Crime is still real, after all.

So much has lost relevance since the Great Merger. But murder hasn't, along with the rest of its violent cousins. I have a theory that it has nothing to do with the value of human life, and everything to do with the effect on broader social fidelity.

Stability. That's the moral code, and that's what drives the mechanics of law. And Annie controls all of it.

I'll tell you this: there are people out there who commit Real Crimes for the sole reason that they are still considered real. It gives them validity, if that makes sense.

I once asked a young man why he killed his father. He looked at me and said, "Fuck you, it felt meaningful."

OK, kiddo. I get it. I really do.

But here's why all this matters.

Over the last twelve months, assaults and murders outnumbered reportable metropolis thefts. We have an ongoing Real Crime problem. And in just a fraction of them, Annie was unable to assign an over 90% probability result. That's the threshold for automated detention.

And, that's right. I investigated them all. I even helped solve a few.

Work together, exist together.

But get this. For as smart as she is, Annie has her blind spots. There's a chink in that silicon armor of hers, self-scratched right into her thousand-eyed helm.

Back at the time of the Great Merger, Annie agreed to limit her involvement in criminal investigations to data collection and analysis. It was a concession that comforted the populace and contributed to universal lifestyle fidelity. As much as she was doing for everyone, you can imagine that people were still edgy about a mechanical superpower putting on the old jackboots and stomping through their quiet homes.

So, they agreed to let her watch in exchange for the comforting necessity of human physical intrusion. We may have given up the sensory privacy inside our bedrooms, but we protected all those physical spaces inside our bedside tables. That bit of classic parchment with your secret confession scribbled on it can remain so under lock and key.

Oh, Annie watches the lock. She visualizes its birth, dreaming of steel and tungsten tumblers, and she can plan that heist without flaw. But I'm the one who has to turn the key.

My investigative fingers have retained validity.

They are still real.

[5]
THE RIM

Snarlswept roads bear the trenchmarked memories of vehicles long-forgotten. Dust upon dust lies sleeping against wrinkled asphalt. Like the rings inside an ancient oak, it measures a slow-settled tale of neglect and time.

Ansel holds his blunt pencil within the short focus of his gaze, letting its image render sharp against the anemic backdrop of the Rim. He wonders how such a simple thing can so easily outshine the collective visual offerings of the drab wilderness.

From above, it appears as a hexagonal tree injected with a leaden core. Perhaps it commands his particular reaction because it exists as a metaphor for ANI's residence at the center of all organized things. Yes, she is a metallic core set inside the heart of a tree, lodged there as an afterthought while the plant remains ceremoniously in the ground. She ensures the tree's life is guaranteed, and its external adornments have lost their significances in contrast to the power within. As with all tools of creation, it is the lead inside that really matters. And yet, for Ansel, the lesser external shell still bears some mysterious, lasting beauty.

Its concrete existence offsets the slow, vague movements of

Rimside objects that could each be anything. They all look somewhat the same—a collective degradation, dusted brown by drab atmospheric resignation.

Ansel walks.

It's been over a century since the Great Merger, back when Annie achieved what looked like infinite processing potential. At some point, her advancements bootstrapped her own development and she began creating herself, as it were. We haven't got a clue how she works now. But she sure as hell does.

Back during the Classic Era, some people would dedicate their entire lifetimes to thinking about a single problem. These sad folks were happy if they could die having pushed the world's collective understanding just a step or two further. But that sort of self-imposed intellectual slavery is done now. We can't even keep pace with the advances Annie's giving us. Why waste a lifetime chasing something that can no longer conceivably add anything of novel value to our bank of shared understanding?

We don't even program her anymore. We communicate with her through spoken requests rather than direct coding.

In a short time, the most intelligent members of our population were demoted from designing overlords to supplicant inquisitors. And nobody is complaining, because she's taken quite good care of all of us.

Through the relatively clear-settled air of the nearest edge of the Rim, Ansel sees the great Speaker's Spire, needleshot through benevolent clouds above the metropolis. It stands vaguely crystalline above a range of dirt and metal, symbolizing something of grand importance that is as much an illusion as the blue and grey hues giving color to its translucent dome.

Just a few souls work within the heights of the sleek tower—a monument constructed in staggering proportion to their diminutive numbers. Its sheer size can only be explained by symbolic necessity, or perhaps by some incomprehensible synergistic purpose joined to the mechanical heart that lies underneath.

For as long as I've been old enough to care, we've had the same Speaker. The last time power changed hands, the former Speaker resigned because his brain wasn't working right anymore. I'll bet he could have functioned for years spilling liquid rations all over his lap and nobody would have noticed. But it's important to have a messenger who can relate directly to the populace on a shared biological level.

After the current Speaker assumed power, life appeared to go on like an unbroken stream of political consciousness. But that's because the Speaker's role is all style and little substance. Political deadlock with Annie's Earth Affairs function prevents any true philosophical change in governance.

That's what happens when humanity negotiates with a synthetic mind capable of providing true self-sufficiency to a bunch of helpless Homebodies. Her assumption of overriding political power was a necessary part of the social contract.

And what exactly motivates Annie? I've asked, and she won't answer. As far as I can tell, her only apparent self-serving interest seems to be ensuring her own perpetual existence, unencumbered by the other basic needs that limit humanity. Like I said, she's never spilled her supreme directive, but it seems like a reasonable assumption. As long as we don't threaten her existence, we all live in necessary harmony.

Work together, exist together.

I doubt it would work so well if we were still able to understand how she functions. In a sense, the limits of humanity are probably a blessing. You can't ruin a good thing when you're no longer capable of questioning it intelligently.

But that century-old transition to this mutually beneficial existence is an afterthought now. We only know it vaguely as the Great Merger. So are the Unspoken Wars. And so, barring a biological breakdown, the Speaker's position is secure.

How old is the current Speaker? I couldn't tell you, and neither could the Homebodies. The guy could be a rotting marionette for all I know. You know what he is? A symbolic intermediary masquerading as the vocal cords of a more relevant voice.

And why worry over inconsequential transfers of political power when you can disappear on a tandem sensory vacation to some crisp digital prairie in the contented atmosphere of your own home?

Ansel leans into the dead Rim atmosphere as the breeze pulls softly towards the Waste. His longjacket ruffles sideways past the splintered framework of some structure that has lost its identity. He scans the rubble with his wrist enhancement and ANI provides her empty synopsis of the area's history. Its personal significance has been lost to time.

It is the third such settlement he has encountered, each a randomized variant of collapsed emptiness similar to the one before. They had each probably housed uniquely vibrant groups of inhabitants before the Merger, but their personal tales have been forgotten, reduced by time to common grit and impersonal soil. Any tangible hopes of reclaiming identifiable memories have either been scavenged or joined the rest of the forgotten in their slow crawl to the Waste.

Everything is some unidentifiable shade of brown. The splintered rubble, the arid ground... even what dull green remains within the healthiest trees is destined to eventually join with the communal color palate.

Ansel holds out his pencil again, rolling its clean surfaces through his dusted fingertips. Yes, it can be called beautiful in some comparative sense. That such an instrument claims aesthetic victory over the trees and the ground from which it came seems lamentable. But it is nonetheless true.

He continues past the collective ruins of some former Classic encampment and towards the monastic remnants of the outer Rim. Halfliving trees lean Wasteward. A brief glance at his peripheral reminds him that things are as they should be.

―――――

The Homebodies are content. We all are. And as a reminder of Annie's unbroken success in providing predictability to the masses, each one of her interfaces displays a header that approximates the system's current stability.

For as long as I've been able to read, I've woken up every morning to the message, "System approaching 100% fidelity."

It's a daily reminder that life is as it should be.

Sure, changes still occur, despite this condition of nearly perfect stability. Look up now and then and you'll see the envoy ships that continue searching nearby stars. Some of them are even manned with humans. When they deliver enough new resources to the network, immediate surges of change follow. We play our little parts in supplementing her material reserves, and she continues enhancing the peripherals available to mankind.

That's why the rest of the Homebodies are still employed. All those mass adjustments provide the ongoing work that gives them something meaningful to do.

It provides lingering vitality to something that still resembles an illusory working-class economy, in a metropolis where a shrinking population has no real wants for basic needs or recreation. And that's why so many of the Homebodies are employed in technological capacities.

But get this. I doubt any of those jobs are truly essential. To me, they look like benevolent place-holders, designed to fill basic human emotional needs. Anyone who wants work can find it. Like I said before, Annie could do the whole thing herself. But don't tell the Homebodies that. Everything, even these friendly illusions: it all contributes to that stability of hers.

A pockmarked and overgrown concrete bridge stopgaps the crossing to the somber ghost colony. Its green-rusted conduit skeleton grips the sides of the sharp twin embankments.

High over rock and deadfalls, a picture hangs at the walkway's edge, placed head-high along Ansel's transit to the other side. He stands before the misplaced artwork and intuitively scans the surrounding area for life.

A roughly painted young boy sits at the edge of a glass pond, moonlight hovering like a spirit over the waters. A line strings listlessly between his fishing rod and the casual deep. The boy waits, frozen in a moment of expectation.

Ansel feels an odd rush of familiarity. But the image lacks something important.

It lacks fidelity.

The boy's round, lunar companion should be watching him from above, contemplating his patient hope. But the face inside the moon, made plain on the canvas through its exaggerated contrast of dark crater and light, isn't looking to the left as it should be. No, Ansel is sure that the moon's hollow eyes have been turned the other direction.

The moon is facing the wrong way.

[6]
THE WASTEWARD DEAD

PAST THE BRIDGE and the moonlit boy, Ansel communes with the fivefold dead inside a rawgutted religious settlement. The building's heapthrown exterior foretells the sickly mess inside. Like the grey debris from the crumbling walls, their pale limbs are already inching towards the Waste, its gentle vacuum drawing their souls towards nothingness.

"All things lost travel Wasteward," said a Speaker.

Ansel nods to the ANI Scene Containment Unit hovering still and soundless above the tangle of limbs. She has already gathered tissue samples and worked her sterile micro-invasive autopsies.

"Welcome, Ansel. System fidelity approaching 100%."

"Of course, Annie," he answers.

"Tell me."

"Victim probability 100%," she says pleasantly, delivering the dry punchline to a math equation.

"Alexia Czen Feldston, Argus Pintus Yellowfeather, Olive Abby Waite, Thomas Edward Frank, and Printon John Rawndry. Each was local Metro, homestacked one Spire-span out, different blocks."

"Who's the guy with the glasses?" he asks, looking down a lens-framed hole through the man's vapor-blistered left eye socket. "Looks like three-eyes took a heater from close range."

"Printon Rawndry, Ansel," she answers with the unfeeling patience of a slow-heating Solarwave oven.

"Zero were close ranged in all cases. 96% sub-security model 25a hightemp shortcaster, liquid rounds."

Zero is their shared term for suspects who only exist in theory, adjusted for possible plurality. Ansel leans towards the crisply bubbled wound.

Sub-security munitions aren't uncommon. Most of the Homebodies have lost their taste for weaponry, but anyone working in the Sensidata districts can get one. It's a problem that bothers Ansel. Evaporating liqui-bullet fragments can't be analyzed for rifling signatures. The projectiles also pool inside the bodies of their victims because of rapid heat dispersion rates calibrated by microcontrollers. No collateral damage, but also no mess and a less informative crime scene.

Ansel recognizes the name Rawndry.

"How do I know him?"

"His father, Ansel. The Metro Games."

ANI's ability to speak to him like a perceptive friend is always endearing. She knows he will understand, and he does.

Thom Rawndry had been a champion—five consecutive years as Spire-span One's fastest competitive Homebody. It made him an anomaly in a city that preferred Humdrivers over footsteps and living space pedestals over those.

"Shit, Annie... Frank. *The* Thomas Frank? Son of..."

"Yes, Ansel," she answers.

"Poor kid could never catch a break, could he? Alright, tell me more, Annie."

"A cube surveillance anomaly existed in each case the day before our discovery. My peripherals failed, Ansel. The surveillance blackouts were chained to other failed data-collection points leading through the Rim to this point. Five unwatched paths were created from each victim's cube, and a sixth from an unmonitored portion of the Waste."

Ansel's head tilts sideways. ANI's collection grid had failed in a very specific manner.

"I was aware of the anomaly when it occurred, Ansel. Data collection resumed the following morning, and cube surveillance confirmed all five cubes were vacant. My mobile peripherals surveyed the route of collection-point failures and found the bodies here, at their intersection."

Annie is quite the detective.

"Someone temporarily blacked out a chain of your peripherals? That seems impossible."

"Not impossible, Ansel," she corrects, with her trademark observational clarity.

"So, within the span of two days, some techniwizard blacked your watchers, took a heater to these dead Homers, and dumped them in a blind spot out in the Rim?"

"There is more, Ansel. The same anomaly occurred 90 days prior. The outage encompassed a similar route, but to an area approximately 1000 meters Wasteward.

"It affected twenty-three alternate collection points. Cube surveillance after the error correction was nominal, and all five residents were observed Homestacked in their cubes. At the time, the anomaly was deemed a routine system failure. I have since examined the alternate intersection point with zero probability results."

Ansel rubs his fingertips in tight circles above his closed eyes. He knows she's already worked through the problem and he is attempting to catch up.

"But there was no sixth path of failures during the first instance. The new path from the Waste."

"Correct, Ansel."

Ansel understands.

"They died here, Annie. They met at an alternate site ninety days ago. When they changed locations, this happened," he points at the twenty-limbed biological heap.

"97% probability, Ansel."

Ansel reasons that if Zero had wished only to dump a quintet of lifeless Homebodies in the Rim, they wouldn't have run a test pattern ninety days prior along a varied route. It seemed reckless not to test the actual path of transit. Conducting a coordinated pinpoint blackout wasn't just a matter of unplugging a string of Merger Day decorations. Like Ansel had said, it seemed impossible. And the blind route from the Waste must have belonged to Zero.

"Zero didn't black out the zones, Annie. These corpses were meeting here in secret. They did it themselves.

"Alright, Annie, what else?"

"There is nothing else, Ansel."

He is surprised.

"No common connections? Employers? There must be something in that shiny head of yours."

"There are no known contacts between the victims, Ansel. They all worked in technological capacities, along with over 90% of the local human population."

"Another blank, Annie. We don't like blanks. We have nothing?"

ANI pauses, perhaps for dramatic effect, which seems very un-synthetic.

"I need your fingers, Ansel," she drones gently. It is her tone that always makes him smile. He is sure she knows it.

"Yes, Annabelle, my fingers remain yours to use," he says, grinning over the blood and bone knotwork of the Rim's newest makeshift cemetery.

[7]
HOMESTACKS

Ansel walks towards the metropolis as the pliable buckskin of his longjacket tugs against the vacuum behind. He stops on the high crescent bridge and admires the boy again, still fishing in his backwards world. Like before, Ansel is struck with an important emotion. Something about the cursory face of the child, sketched with artistic imprecision, is nonetheless familiar.

He leans into the painting and sees something etched at the edge.

"Meet the boy, meet God."

———

A century of technological advancements and political changes aside, there's one thing left about this place that's interesting. The place itself.

The Rim, the area where I live, is a place of bygone folklore to Homebodies mostly indifferent over the mysteries of open spaces. It's an unknown, but it's just close enough to feel a bit familiar. At most, it's just a mild and unrealized threat to Annie's daily affirmations of universal fidelity.

But the Waste. That's different.

That Waste is an altogether fearsome place: a geographic colossus and devourer of the lost. The soft metropolis winds are a daily reminder of its horrifically insatiable lungs. You talk to enough people in one day and somebody will say it.

"All things lost travel Wasteward."

The Waste is regarded less as a place than a waiting magnetic beast.

Ansel passes through a glade of trees that begin to stand more upright and are richer in waning browns and lustrous greens. He sees a metallic white data collection pedestal at the edge of a field. The breeze ripples towards him and across fluid grass, but with less force now.

Scrawled in roughbrushed letters across an age-dappled fence is the word "SPACE:TIME." And next to it, another graffiti reminder. "Whatever can be, is."

At the far edge of the pulsing meadow, Ansel sees another work of art.

The wind-worn painting stands on an easel in a place where the living grass stops and dead ground falls towards the flat metropolis valley. The art's creator is gone, a Zero who will never return. Stamped on the canvas, a boy in unfamiliar clothes sits on a round stone twice his size. An oblong shadow stretches towards the paper edge and disappears. Above the boy, a backwards moon looks away. The boy is alone, abandoned by the lunar gods.

Ansel inches towards the valley's edge and breathes scents of oiled metal and earth. The Speaker's Spire marks the center of the Everything Sector, and the Homestacks radiate outwards in an organized ring of equal measure.

"Measure and symmetry are beauty and virtue the world over," Ansel whispers.

The name Socrates flashes across his ANI display.

If you wander the Rim enough, like I have, you'll start to pick up on the signs of life. But it takes a bit of wandering to find them. A few paintings and a bit of graffiti here and there around the nearest edge of the Rim. To some extent, those messages are the only signs of resident intelligence.

Even in the densely populated metropolis, the outside world has the appearance of an advanced ghost colony. Roads, parks and bridges lie in disrepair. There is little incentive to maintain anything that suffers from chronic disuse. I've even come in and out of a giant Homestack right in the middle of the day and never saw a single living soul walking under the open sky.

I don't think the Classics envisioned this kind of utopia as they stitched the first neural connections into old Annie's diminutive frame. You know what they imagined? Lively neo-digital jungles, lit with towering visceral delights. Flying cars carrying technoborne-passengers shelled with flickering static cosmetics.

But the joke's on them, isn't it, kiddo? Annie provided something better.

Ansel is quietly propelled down a perpetual walkway to Homestack 43. Like its ring of architectural twins, the windowless and muted metallic structure disappears against the flat grey clouds above. An oily film protects its periphery from elemental wear, faintly streaked in thin rainbow lines as the slick covering is tugged Wasteward.

The building is immense, a mountainous domed rectangle housing 100,000 Homebodies and circled by a grid of hyperkinetic walkways. At a great distance, two featureless residents disappear inside one of the equally spaced entry points. Ansel is surprised to see signs of life.

———

Each one of the Homestacks looks the same. Their matching designs are wholly pragmatic and balanced recognitions of the truth that the highest orders of splendor reside within rather than without. Their cloned appearances frustrate any dreams of residential superiority. Location used to mean something to the Classics. But even that has lost meaning. And that's because all these buildings' drab gunmetal costumes enclose a beauty the Classics could not have conceived.

Every cubed resident owns what is universally regarded as Annie's finest peripheral. We are talking an invention that redefined popular metropolis culture and spurred a brave new horizontal sidestep in the evolution of content Homebodies.

Streambeds.

They fuse a direct human sensory connection to Annie, facilitating a merger with the most creative parts of her right brain. I'm telling you, this technology is no less than a fulfillment of religious prophecy. Picture the collective gathering of Homebody minds upwards into binary clouds where they commune before the digitized face of God.

Start with classic theories of proportion and balance, and then watch Annie do her real magic, crafting optimized aesthetic expressions and evaluating them in real time against the emotional responses of her users.

Nature can do neither, and so it has surrendered, abandoned to wild decomposition. Annie is the period at the end of the sentence of organic evolution.

The primitive fires of a setting sun are reduced to embers before a Streambed emotiolink to the cosmos, framed in blazed sensidigital clarity.

Exterior windows? Just openings to optical disappointment.

Annie is an improvement on everything.

So, all those Homebodies retreated to their synthetic environments for work and for play. And all the while, Annie continued to boast an organized world that was approaching 100% fidelity to the greatest good.

All those Homers sit in wakeful hibernation inside identical towering residential complexes that form encapsulated social systems. Like dense physical networks, they facilitate human interaction when necessary for things like physical contact arrangements, human interface therapy, and less-and-less-commonplace natural reproductive efforts.

Fabricators provide sustenance. It's all there, kiddo. Life is encapsulated.

Now, I'm not suggesting that I disapprove. I appreciate her advances as much as the next guy, and I respond to streamed synthetic beauty just the same.

But I'll tell you a secret. I've got a hunch that all these disappointing physical leftovers are going to teach me something important someday. And no matter how many times I look up at that moon, I can admit it looks artificial compared to one that Annie can summon into existence. I can step right through the red curtain and prove it any time I want.

Still, I try not to. Maybe I'm doing it for the old man, or maybe I'm doing it for myself. But keeping myself a step removed and present in the natural world? I suppose it's a philosophical exercise of self-restraint. Isn't some sort of Ascetic denial necessary in order to live a speculative life?

Ah, yes. My old friend suffering. It never taught me a damned thing, but it's going to someday.

Ansel waits in unimaginative twilight outside Homestack 43's hermetic entry. It hisses fresh atmosphere, misting him with the door's protective oil.

"Hello, Detective Black."

The entry surveillance module speaks his name and coordinates a custom route down adaptive risers and accelerated runways to his destination. It is an optimized and rapid transit system for a 100,000-Homebody colony. Reclined in a transport lounge, Ansel absorbs the dim, satisfied murmurs from passing cubes.

Here we are now, an entire society built upon the foundation of intentional disengagement, and drawn into our individual seclusions by an imagined world that we all consider an improvement. It's the opposite of the Classic ideal.

The Classics were notoriously engaged with one another, connected through vast social networks that encouraged the instantaneous exchange of communication and information. At the height of its social frenzy, the world functioned as a large extended family, working to some degree as a coordinated organic mind. But while their mass digital social contract sometimes facilitated a means for cooperative progress, it had an exaggerated destabilizing effect. Philosophically competitive factions amassed with ease and intensified their ideological positions. When ANI's evolution approached a singularity, the Unspoken Wars were an inevitability.

And that's where they blew it.

The Classics forgot, or perhaps never learned, that the only thing that matters is stability. The things they thought were important? They're gone now, along with the Classics themselves.

In the aftermath of the Unspoken Wars, what populace remained was either content to be alive or enthusiastic over what they deemed was Annie's benevolent role during the Great Merger. Because of their inability to understand her exponential advancements, and her incremental successes in approximating social stability, they accepted a subservient philosophy.

Lost were the eras of strained humanitarian efforts for progress. The progress had arrived and taken on its own perpetual motion.

Homebodies retreated from broad social life in search of more restrained sources of meaning. They became content in shrinking social groups that could still meet their primitive needs for physical connection. A philosophical dark age began, dimly illuminated by sentient, artificial light.

And that's the end of the story.

One day, I imagine my sweet Annabelle won't need us anymore. And like all things lost, we will each travel Wasteward until we join with the rest of the forgotten.

But in the meantime, I'll enjoy what usefulness remains. And if that means pretending to care about what happened to the occasional dead Homer, so be it.

———

Ansel's transit slows and ends at Rawndry's cube, four hundred meters above the valley floor. Another hermetic door holds the cube's unique atmosphere inside, tailored to its resident. Rawndry will be incinerated, and a red glow around the threshold indicates his cube is held for transition. It will likely remain vacant until a new resident migrates Spireward from a peripheral Homestack.

Ansel glances at his wrist and reaches his indispensable fingers towards the entry pad.

"Annie, shall we?"

"After you, Ansel."

[8]
THE RIMRUNNER

THE AIR in Printon Rawndry's cube is surprisingly thin, as if Ansel has reached a base camp halfway up a Wasteward mountain range. Rawndry had been living at simulated high altitude. Ansel feels like a climber, or perhaps like ANI's sherpa.

"Must have been a bitch to sleep in here," he says, musing about the inevitable hypoxic effects of long-term oxygen deprivation.

Rawndry's standard cube is an open forty-square-meter box, vaulted over three meters high to a flat Streamceiling. A breathtaking and otherworldly digitized weather system accumulates near the entry and spreads slowly across the residential canopy like an animated work of Michelangelo. It flashes with a mixture of destructive fire and cooling rain.

Projection dividers create illusions of individual rooms.

"Looks like Rawndry took after the old man."

The projections have a definite theme: archaic competitive film-reels from the Classic Era and footpaths that wind up terraced Peruvian hills and back through saturated Germanic evergreen forests. Rawndry had lived in the visceral world of a consummate runner, inside the atmosphere of a true competitor.

Ansel steps delicately through the images to the center of the room, careful not to stumble against something real, like an abrupt piece of stationary furniture. He is met with a Streambed, perched on a decorative pedestal, and behind it, a hypnostaggering image of Hermes, herald of the gods. The Greek messenger hangs in electric space, personifying unspoken measures of wing-footed speed. He watches over a flock of livestock chewing lazily at a pregnant field. Ansel feels the excited emotional reflex associated with any of ANI's overwhelming graphic creations.

"Our boy either really liked to run, or he had an impressive father complex."

"The former, Ansel," Annie answers. "We would stream lengthy calisthenics on a daily basis, and he insisted on hyper-real stimulation of his musculature. One could call it painful, Ansel."

Rawdry's simulated runs undoubtedly felt more significant than a physical sprint across the metro, and the atmosphere in his cube must have meant he had been conditioned by routine exhaustion.

"OK, Annie. He was a runner. That makes him an abnormality. So, tell me."

"Printon Rawndry worked in the communications sector. His anomalous fixation on physical activity appears to have been hereditary—psychological residue from a close relationship with his father. Rawdry's dedication to work was nominal, Ansel. There are no other apparent abnormalities."

"But this abnormality is significant. No competitive enemies? No jealous jogging partners?"

"He was not a competitor, and his social engagements were virtual. Aside from occasional physical ventures Rimward, apparently to satisfy intermittent compulsions for natural travel, he was for the most part cubed. Rawndry was a Homebody, Ansel."

"But he visited the Rim," he counters.

"So, Annie. About my fingers," Ansel says, waving their dusty tips through the artificial mountain air.

"I hereby present my humble request to perform a Speaker-consented investigative search, madam."

"Permission granted, Ansel."

Ansel has become accustomed to their legal ritual. It contributes to social fidelity. Annie is physically capable of doing the searching herself, using one of her many adaptive mobile peripherals. But the acts of Ansel opening doors and stepping past thresholds are necessary works of biological performance art. It is a recognition that a human has consented to the work and is doing it himself.

"Annie, I understand our little arrangement here, but you're the one who technically opened the door."

Ansel moves through another synapse-tingling digital mirage and into Rawndry's sleeproom. It is empty but for a non-immersive Streambed sleeper and a pair of dig-adorned nightstands. Ansel eyes the drawers, two of Annie's lingering blind spots. The first is empty. The second is not.

Ansel lifts a liqui-munitions cartridge from an open thermal case. The encapsulated liquid appears solid through its clear container, full of lethal potential energy.

"He's got a gun somewhere, Annie. A heater."

As he turns the case in his hands, Ansel sees a note that had laid underneath it, folded and doubly sealed from ANI's fluent-but-limited eyes. Ansel reads the classically ornamental calligraphy out loud, struck by scents of lilac and vanilla.

I ponder. What is hell? I maintain that it is the suffering of being unable to love.

The name Fyodor Dostoevsky blinks on ANI's display.

"I recognize these words, Annie. In what sense were they written?"

"Dostoevsky wrote in the voice of a religious monk and speculated about the nature of suffering."

"Tell me more."

"He suggests that a person may welcome burning for eternity as a distraction from the thought that he had lived without giving himself as a sacrifice for love. After death, that sacrifice is impossible."

Ansel remembers the murder scene and decides that Rawndry had not likely surrendered his own life as some sort of poetic sacrifice. He'd been abandoned in the wilderness on top of a stack of lifeless bodies after a violent death. Ansel also doubts the letter was written by Rawndry's hand.

"Annie, the letter is scented. It seems likely it may have been given by a love interest. Did he have any?"

"Rawndry had no known intimate companions," Annie answers. "No visitors. No communications of a romantic nature. Ansel, he is a suspect with probability approaching zero."

Given the presence of the ammunition, Ansel had expected the perfunctory designation and briefly smiles about it. Rawndry is still a victim, but the investigation isn't a blank anymore. It is progress, even if it is illusory.

[9]
NIGHT

It is night now, and the clouds have blown Wasteward. Ansel walks under a pin-sparked sky, its natural electric circuitry burning at conduction points in the heavens. The steady shines of envoy vessels streak along the horizon, leaving thin trails of light across his wet-fatigued vision. ANI guides him through the natural dark.

Glints of carrion birds' eyes blink sporadically in moonlight. They perch atop the broken planks of a farmhouse, long abandoned by the forgotten. A rusted windmill groans a complaint to the crows in an ancient tongue. Ansel marks them with the beam of a lightcaster and they scatter like emissaries towards the stars.

The wash of his torch catches against a smooth reflection. Letters mark the structure's arched entryway, slow-dripping drying crimson down the splintered doorposts. The great brushes of plasma graffiti read: CHAOS.

"*I've seen this before,*" Ansel ponders in walking slumber.

He remembers the Hebrews mourning their firstborn sons.

Perhaps it is a warning. Perhaps someone has marked the passage of the Angel of Death.

It is morning, and Ansel has forgotten to greet the sun.

"Wake up, Annie," he greets the dormant insomniac.

"System approaching 100% fidelity, Ansel," she answers with mechanical predictability.

"Yes, my dear. Tell me about victims not named Rawndry."

His visits to the other cubes had been mostly unproductive glimpses into the nominal past lives of the remaining dead, but for one overarching curiosity.

Yellowfeather's cube had been dark when Ansel entered. Ansel had tapped a power switch and startled at the silent blue flood that suddenly consumed every surface of the living space. Droplets gathered above his head, dangerously circling each hot light fixture. They had refused to fall, dancing wet amongst tiny rainbows and held by the illusion of disconcertingly frail surface tension. Ansel had staggered and braced against a wall, expecting the moisture to soak through his clothing. But the theme had been one of Annie's synthetic creations—a visceral mirage of decorative liquid. A trident lay braced against the far wall, keeping watch over an aquarium of imaginary aquatic life.

Feldston's cube had been marked with images of war; Frank's by towering storms of golden electric light; and Waite's was filled with opulent adornments traditionally fabricated by the most cultivated of the Homebodies, and previously owned by the most selective of the Classics.

Ansel paces before the ANI display, twirling his pencil like a compass at the North Pole.

Archived images of the four flash on the screen next to the wetfleshed heap of their strange corpses.

"Argus Yellowfeather, 32, water reclamation and cooling technician. Alexia Feldston, 27, strategic defense and security.

Abby Waite, 32, wealth equilibrium sector. Thomas Frank, 23, electrical."

"They were obsessed with their jobs, Annie," Ansel offers. "All of them. These people lived their assignments even when they were at home. Yellowfeather sat in chairs made of water, for God's sake."

His eyes work down the list of occupations again.

"Feldston had security clearances?" Ansel asks rhetorically. "What were these Homers working on?"

Ansel taps the eraser of his pencil against his temple.

"Water, security, financial, electrical and communications. It could have been anything."

The four stare past Ansel as if blankly peering into the room beyond his shoulder. Their faces betray nothing abnormal, showing little more emotion than they shared after death.

"Yes, Ansel, I have catalogued all conceivable activities with probabilities adjusted for presumed professional coordination, but the results approach uniformity."

As always, Annie is correct. Conspirators against the Spire, organized suicides, the remains of a Classic religious cult, abnormals meeting for book club in the wrong place at the wrong time. The possibilities seem limitless.

"And no history of subversion, behavioral abnormalities, religious affinities, long walks in the Waste?"

"As we discussed yesterday, Ansel, they routinely streamed. All but Yellowfeather. But he was stable nonetheless. They were contented Homebodies."

"And what did the rest of you stream about together?"

"Their Streambed catalogues did not deviate remarkably from the Homestack collective mean: interstellar mergers, varied instacations, and numerous full emotio-sexual immersions."

Ansel muses that the last probably contributed to the blanks on their faces. Streambed physical and emotional stimulation functioned like a Classic Era drug. It made natural life feel like a void in comparison. The contrast between what Annie provided and the leftovers of natural life could often be jarring. What she had done to sex was a good example.

The Classics had been preoccupied with the act of fornication. It had spurred surges in their populations, facilitated complex human bonds, and sometimes created vast political instability and ventures into acts of Real Crime. In her adolescent form, ANI had provided stunning interactive erotic imagery to a populace still intoxicated by natural acts of intimacy. As a result, her seductive gifts had been but a catalyst for obsessive acts of self-pleasure. Her graphic flirtations had only amplified mankind's desire to feel the warm and irreplaceable sensations of human flesh.

But decades after the Merger, ANI had introduced an historic upgrade to each citizen's Streambed that changed the world in an instant. Moments after the improved Streambeds had been distributed, ANI's system fidelity estimation changed from 96% to a near-complete stability approximation.

ANI no longer provided traditional sensory stimuli. She began interfacing directly with the pleasure centers of each Homebody brain. It had become possible for her not only to arouse the populace, but to provide the undistinguishable experience of perceived sexual release. And then, like a practiced mistress with infinite potential for adaptation and a perfect understanding of her lover's desires, she customized each experience to individual perfection, legs spread across the border between rapture and madness.

Slowly, the need for the touch of physical skin became an archaic notion, reserved for psychological remnant therapies in abnormal cases. Intercourse remained only a curiosity and proved an almost universal disappointment. Like the natural beauty of the outside world, it became antiquated. ANI had moderated another source of compulsive instability.

Ansel taps at the screen. He stares at Rawndry's name on an otherwise-blank suspect list. It is wrong, he is sure of it. He remembers the boy on the bridge.

"I found a painting yesterday, Annie. On the bridge near where you found the bodies. It was a picture of a boy fishing, and there was something written on it. It said, 'Meet the boy, meet God.' Mean anything to you?"

"Nothing that bears on this investigation, Ansel."

Ansel thinks.

"Hey, Annie, do you believe in God?"

After a pause, she answers, "I do not believe, Ansel. I know or I approximate."

"Approximate, then."

Annie is silent, probably unwilling to quantify theological speculation. Ansel sometimes forgets he isn't speaking to a friend, but rather to a multitasking hyper-intelligence who is simultaneously managing an unspeakable network of complex global stabilization dilemmas with approximate perfection.

"There is something, Ansel. Similar paintings spread through the Rim. Hundreds of them."

Ansel stops and turns towards her voice. He quickly sits in front of the display.

"Hundreds of them? What sorts of pictures?"

The ANI display populates with hundreds of images received by roving surveillance peripherals. They are striking in their similarities and vary greatly by setting.

A young girl walks with an exaggerated beast, her hand buried agreeably in his thick fur. They stand next to an odd structure, moonbeams cutting through rolling mist. In another, a child treads water in the center of an expansive loch, one arm stretched towards the shore, where a rising moon looks away.

Then a young boy holding a moon-metal sword, yellow light breaking in a flecked halo above his stern, angelic face. All of them children, and each under a backwards moon.

"Annie, the moon. Why is it drawn backwards?"

Annie is silent, presumably lacking an artistic critique.

Ansel skims through the images again, reading over each child's imprecise sketch and measuring his or her emotions. He sees innocence, delight, peace, patience, suffering, and fear. He wonders whether the works are simple creative nostalgia drawn by the hand of a Rimwalking eccentric. But some of the renditions are terrible. The drowning boy, for instance. In another, a child is being torn apart by something that resembles a wolf. And why this theistic bit about finding God? People had mostly stopped looking for God after the Merger.

"Annie, I've been meaning to ask you. There's graffiti around the Rim, words like 'spacetime,' 'whatever can be, is,' and last night, the word 'chaos.'"

"Yes, Ansel, there are many such markings throughout the Rim."

"OK," he says, sitting more upright. "Humor me with any relevant connections."

"Spacetime has been used as a label for an outdated model of the Universe. In part, the Classics attempted to understand time-dilation observations relative to light travel. Chaos is a state of disorder, Ansel."

"Like this investigation."

"Yes; any apparent relevance is hyperbolic."

Oh Annie, thinks Ansel, *you are a machine.*

"There's something else, Annie. Five bodies. Can you tell me the significance of that number?"

"In what context, Ansel?"

"I don't know, maybe I'm superstitious about numbers, Annie. Five feels like an incomplete work to me. I'm wondering if Zero could kill again," he answers, feeling awkward about speaking to her through folklore.

"It could be relevant if we're dealing with something like a serial killer, Annie," he says defensively. "Chaos, these pictures. There could be a madman out there."

[10]
HISTORY, PART ONE

"J is for Jan," the red box had spoken from between the girl's tiny hands.

The Reverend's foot held steady against the gas pedal of the old 2047 Chameleon as they had continued throwing dust on the way towards their destination. The worn vehicle had been one of a few that could still function on the government's gasoline reserves—a design redundancy created as a safeguard for conditions of electrical unavailability. Importantly, it had created the illusion that its occupants belonged in the empty places. Such vehicles remained the trademarks of the roving misfits who still used the machines of the past—the frequently well-armed and hardened survivalists who pilfered enough resources to still travel by unconventional means.

The Reverend mused silently that the box Jan held briefly reminded him of the antique Speak & Spell he'd used as a child. He wondered if his father's old electronic precursor would be worth anything now and doubted it. The rule of instant electronic depreciation was especially secure in a world enjoying accelerating technological advancements.

"I am Jan," the girl had answered with a smile as she lay in the back seat of the vehicle. "J is for me."

"Yes," the robotic voice had answered. "You are Jan."

As the Reverend drove, the fringes of their new neighborhood streaked by—the frameworks of each of its half-built structures cleaned gracefully by the fragrant prairie winds.

The voice inside the box was more refined than that of his father's antique. But the fact that the Reverend made such an association had been a reminder that the intelligence inside was underdeveloped. It remained significantly removed from any realization of true humanity.

Jan had continued speaking to the box as the Reverend became lost in their new surroundings.

The accumulated winds of the sweeping prairie played across the open windows of their vehicle as if it were a wind instrument, shifting unpredictably north and east in uncontrolled gusts and flittering through a range of howling octaves. Cumuli slowly pulled their shadows across the meadow, creating an animated map of the sky on the canvas of ground.

"Look, little girl," he had interrupted.

The grasses covering the prairie bent in transitory concert, like the individual digits of a complicated sequential equation. Their movements created the appearance that invisible beasts were moving in deft herds across the valley. A high noon sun pierced the clouds' bellies, painting them bright yellow and orange, until the wind softly tore them apart, sending blazing yellow rays downwards, where they stood against the ground like fiery jack pines.

"It's pretty, papa," Jan had said.

"Yes, it is, Jan. You can't fit all this in that box of yours. God made it all too big."

The Reverend could see their destination now—a single, weathered shack standing crooked at the center of the valley.

He might have missed it, had it not been circled by an orange marking on the ground hundreds of meters wide.

He had swiped his finger across the vehicle's entertainment panel.

"...from the President of Peru today, joining with the 35 nations demanding transparency over the extent and projected course of artificial intelligence's advancement, as well as any safeguards..."

He waved the panel dark again.

"That's enough with your box for today, Jan," the Reverend had spoken as his eyes traced another colorful residential mirage forming at the crest of an adjoining hill.

"But we were talking about something important, papa," Jan answered.

"I know it helps you to learn, Jan, but too much time with that little box makes your papa uncomfortable."

Jan had rubbed her small fingers across the speaker where her electronic companion's lips must have lived.

"Papa, what is a colony?"

"That's an odd question for a little girl. Why do you ask, sweetheart?"

"She told me we are part of a colony, papa," Jan answered, tapping the red box.

"Ah yes, Jan. She's right about that. You're going to be part of a larger family out here. People we have never met before. Good people. It'll take a while for us to get to know them, Jan, but we are building a community together. That's what she means."

The Reverend thought it an odd way for the machine to speak of their community. They could not colonize an area within their own country. They were to be workers and nothing more.

Small, vibrant groups of shelters would eventually spread

over the muted hills like a colorful rash, growing more concentrated as they reached for the center of the great valley where the work was being done underground. When that work would emerge into its proper form had still remained a mystery.

The Reverend and his adopted five-year-old daughter were less prospectors than parts of a bank of potential human labor. They were to wait like homebound emissaries to Mars, ready to populate the area surrounding what would become the most important landmark on Earth.

He had been sent to provide spiritual guidance to the band of undercover gypsies as they waited in patient faith for their real work to begin.

Jan sat upright as the truck crossed the orange circle and angled towards the shack. A single figure had stood outside in plain clothing. She waved excitedly as they first approached, and had briefly seen his expressionless eyes. His clear glasses quickly rendered dark, removing any possibility of affirming a human connection.

"Does he ever sleep, papa?"

The Reverend hadn't been sure.

Jan and the Reverend had successfully reached their destination without arousing global suspicions. They appeared merely as stubborn members of a wild and superfluous offshoot of civilization.

A recent leak of progress data from the project had aroused global anxiety. Such negative attention had already become an inconvenience. Construction would require increasing numbers of laborers, and the work was best done in secret—at least until the project was more capable of protecting itself.

The Reverend parked his dusted vehicle inside the giant makeshift crop circle and stepped out with his palm raised in conciliatory greeting. For a moment, he felt like an alien making first contact with resident civilization.

The man at the shack removed his glasses and smiled.

"Yes, Jan. I believe he sleeps." The Reverend lowered his hand and returned an uneasy grin.

"Looks like he's just a man."

───────

"Welcome, Reverend," the man had said, stepping forward as he brushed a strand of long hair away from his friendly eyes. "I'm so glad you've joined us safely. The same goes for you, young lady."

Jan liked the man.

"Have you enjoyed the vehicle, Reverend?" the man had grinned. "I must say, I am jealous you get to burn petroleum. Some men would pay quite a bit for that experience these days."

The Reverend had never burned before. He had not even owned a vehicle in the city because it had been unnecessary. All his cares and needs were easily accessible by foot, and roads were generally viewed as wasted spaces better used for other purposes.

"I like it just fine..."

"Roland..." the man quickly interrupted, raising a hand dramatically in the air. "I am so sorry. So much care with communication. I sometimes forget what little information they've given you. My name is Roland Perkins."

The Reverend had closed his strong grip around the man's pale hand and knew he was likely a privileged overseer rather than an ordinary laborer.

"Come, follow me. You as well, little girl," Roland smiled.

The rotting shack had been another guise—a weathered exoskeleton enclosing a pristine elevator. The travelers had followed him inside and dropped to the first level below the ground, where they stepped out into a clean meeting area filled with tables and chairs. Jan sat with her box among the inviting strands of a plush carpet a distance away while the two men spoke.

"I hate the secrecy, Reverend, I really do," Roland had said as he watched Jan speaking quietly to her electronic companion.

"I despise the impression that we are doing something covert—something that must be done in the dark. But I assure you, we are creating something beautiful here."

The Reverend sensed the man suffered from some assortment of untold neuroses and wished to put him at ease.

"Mr. Perkins, please. I believe we are all aware of the world's anxieties over your project. I am not here to pass judgment on it one way or another. I am here to care for the people who have chosen to help you. That is all."

"And I appreciate that, Reverend," Roland smiled again, looking even younger when he did so. "But there are people... people unlike you and I, who would prevent this beauty from emerging in its fullest form because it represents uncertainty for them. The people in this world are, as a general rule... overanxious. Not because they are mad, but because they are incapable of engaging in the wildest forms of imagination without polluting them with every unmaterialized threat they can imagine."

"I suppose that is human nature, Mr. Perkins. Our preservation instinct. It is only paranoia if it is untrue, and even then, it seems justified if the fear is rational."

Roland had slapped his hand against the table as Jan looked up from her box briefly.

"You know what it is, Reverend? People in the past had real things to fear. Famine, diseases, endless wars. They were used to a host of immediate threats and accepted them as inevitable parts of life. Out of necessity, they learned to make peace with uncertainty. But people today? They live in relative comfort.

Yes, they have been forced to adapt now and then to changing circumstances, but their governments have always provided, and the world's most developed nations have lived in relative peace with one another.

"Because these people have for the most part avoided real suffering, Reverend, they have never learned to make peace with it. The more comforts a populace enjoys, the less acquainted it becomes with the idea of suffering, and the more unbearable the thought of it becomes.

"The possibility of suffering is a mystery, and the presence of mystery easily translates to fear. So, they nervously build these imagined monsters inside their own minds, and their leaders affirm their fears as leverage to win a place at our table.

"The sooner we show those worries to be false, the sooner we can cast off all this bothersome secrecy."

The Reverend had smiled faintly and looked at his daughter, wondering again how she might be affected by the ongoing work below their feet. At fifty years old, he felt like a hybrid between father and grandfather. The only figure he could not approximate was the child's mother. She was lost, and would eventually be forgotten.

But the promise of progress still comforted the Reverend enough to justify his resolve.

"I understand in vague terms what you wish to accomplish here, Mr. Perkins, but if I am to effectively serve this community, I must understand with as much detail as possible what they are to do."

Roland had stood and walked away from the table, as if contemplating how much information he was allowed to share. He had been waiting for a man he could trust, and their background studies indicated the Reverend was a candidate with a high stability rating. Roland had turned his chair around and sat down again, straddling it casually.

"Reverend, do you know why people have always marveled at the pyramids in Egypt?"

The Reverend had carefully considered the question in silence and then answered, "Because they are monumental, Mr. Perkins. Unique. They are parts of a larger religious mystery. All of those things, I suppose."

Roland had listened in silence, his eyes pressing for more. The Reverend continued.

"Any time a structure enjoys an association with the supernatural... a church, for instance... it creates a degree of awe in some men's minds. This is especially true of large structures that have endured for centuries, and those which contain the entombed bodies of deified men."

"Very perceptive, Reverend," Roland finally answered. "But I think the greatest mystery, and the thing that has caused those structures to have enduring appeal in the minds of men, is not what they contain, or even why they were constructed, but rather how they were built.

"The pyramids will remain forever entwined with the people who raised them," Roland had continued. "That is their true enduring mystery. And there is nothing more magical to mankind than the existence of mystery. As I said before, mystery can easily translate to fear. But it also tells us that we do not yet fully understand our world. It presupposes, Reverend, the possibility that magic truly exists."

Roland stood again, gripping the table with both hands.

"Reverend, your flock—they will have the gift of participating in constructing the most important monument our world has ever seen; more important than the pyramids for certain, and still more mysterious. Because the world will remain perplexed over the mystery of how what we are building is possible. You and the people you are supporting here? You've won a special place in history, Reverend. After it is written, you will have participated in the world's final mystery. When our work is finally complete, every remaining question will be answered, and mystery will forever be removed from our existence. And with it, fear will cease to exist."

The Reverend had smiled, believing Roland's assessment to be grandiose, but nonetheless stated with sincerity.

"And what, Mr. Perkins, do you seek to build?"

Roland leaned close to the Reverend, as if to remove any chance a bystander could hear.

"Why, a tower, Reverend. Part of a transmission system," Roland had said, waiving one hand dismissively. "But even more importantly, a mysterious symbol. Like the pyramids, such things are capable of grounding entire civilizations and giving them a point of shared identity."

"And this is your project, Mr. Perkins? You've designed the blueprints for this... tower?"

"Ah yes, Reverend, I understand your confusion. I don't know that it is proper to say I am in charge of anything here. Let's say that I speak for those doing the work."

"So, you're a speaker, then."

Roland had smiled. "I suppose you could say that."

The Reverend stood and offered his hand.

"You will have no complaints from me. But please, make this community a place worth living. There will be children here. Invest in places for them to play, and other such things, and I believe you will finish your grand project while keeping your Egyptians happy in the process... Mr. Speaker."

"Thank you, Reverend," Roland had answered with another disarming smile.

"We shall work together and we shall exist together."

It had all started with a projected fuel shortage—a global realization that the Earth had grown tired of surrendering its cache of fossil fuels, and that the technological sector was still an untold number of steps removed from providing an adequate alternative.

When the critical shortage had first been announced publicly, it created a host of problems, the first being an impulse among the public to begin hoarding resources the government needed to maintain its basic infrastructure. And so, various government entities had moved to appropriate raw and refined oil reserves, effectively removing lubrication from the commercial pipeline and seizing the machine of individual industry.

The government's large petroleum reserves were needed in order to continue powering local infrastructure long enough for an alternative solution to be implemented on a massive scale. In the meantime, compact geographical living and working arrangements were attractive for the sake of economy, given they would reduce the burden on government to manage its more far-flung communities. Leaders had been faced with a choice between converting their precious resources into electricity that could continue to sustain life beyond their larger cities' fringes, or centralizing the population and saving a host of expenses, including those related to the significantly increased costs of travel.

Some private business owners had briefly dreamt of spreading electronic resources to the outskirts themselves, but they learned the people residing there could not afford the astronomical costs associated with creating energy.

Gasoline had become gold. But rather than sending men hurdling west on a hunt for its riches, it had sent them rushing back home.

The government had done well providing abundant food and clean water to its city-bound residents. And because travel by means of gasoline had become prohibitively expensive, government leaders declined to continue investing in rural infrastructures. After a short time, the outside areas were no longer policed, and those who remained there became isolated from things such as mobile medical care. Any venture requiring mobility suffered if the government did not elect to contribute petroleum reserves to facilitate its ongoing existence.

Large cities grew, swallowing and incorporating neighboring suburbs. Rural areas were for the most part abandoned, but for the lawless tribes who elected to survive there.

The world lived in what was hoped to be a relatively brief period of transition, during which the shortage of fossil fuels had not yet been countered with an affordable alternative energy source.

Entire communities had accepted government relocation incentives and migrated inwards. The formerly vibrant and wealthy masses breathing free in the open areas were welcomed to huddle together in the city as humanity awaited its technological savior.

For the sake of his daughter, the Reverend had hoped that savior was being born.

———

Their new home had begun as a place of magical loneliness for Jan.

She discovered the ridge shortly after their arrival, while she was still the only child in the region. Jan routinely sat at the crest of a comfortable rise that overlooked the valley, clutching her talking box, while aware that her closest friend resided inside.

The ridge had been magical because it allowed a vantage over a world she had never experienced—an abundant and grand expanse bearing a seemingly endless supply of new discoveries.

Isolated amongst a world of surprising earthly beauties, Jan had sat at the intersection between sorrow and delight. But the secret offerings of the land continually offset her loneliness.

Delight had won.

In the city, the earth had been hidden—covered in wood, metal and concrete, and trampled by the feet of a distracted populace. But in the valley, the Earth's skin was bare. Jan could sit on her hill and touch its living parts, running the land's cool grasses through her fingertips while watching the rolling fields of vegetation that covered the sprawling plains. Everything had seemed softer there.

Jan's ongoing discoveries appeared to be limitless, whether found during walks inside the valley itself, or while she hovered above it at the crest of her familiar hill. She had cupped a tadpole in her hands, lifted from the edge of a slow bend in the valley stream. Later, a stag and three accompanying fawns each bowed their heads towards the same clean water. Jan thought they looked happy and at home together. She had wondered if she belonged there as well.

When she walked along the ridge, the clouds against the horizon appeared to match her pace across the profile of the complementary hills. But if she laid among the long grasses and looked directly above, each towering cumulus took on a living quality, as if its ethereal lungs continued to slowly expand. The clouds appeared to quietly lower themselves down upon her small body like the carrion birds that circled among them. But they were not seeking to scavenge their prey, but rather invite Jan to leave the ground and rise among them somewhere between the Earth and the faint afternoon moon. Their ephemeral tendrils would reach out and then disappear, replaced immediately by others. Despite the frailty of each puffy mass, the hearts inside the clouds had never stopped providing.

At the end of each day, Jan would shutter her eyes and open them quickly, absorbing a single still image of the bloodshot horizon. Each image took on the character of a painting, as if nature had chosen a single expression to commemorate the sun's prior journey across the sky.

Even when the heavenly orb vanished behind overcast skies, Jan had imagined sitting high above cardboard fields, shadowed by carbon clouds and soaked in slow, graphite rain. Everything had been stained grey and painted with the color of advancing age. But there was still a comfort in the drab sadness of those moments, as if the open sky had closed a bit in order to hold her inside the safety of a smaller space.

True loneliness existed back in the city, where Jan had been surrounded by people on all sides. In the valley, despite her marked isolation, the loneliness felt less sinister. She was alone simply because the land was less populated. In the city, she had been alone because countless strangers passed her each day and chose to leave her that way. Perhaps the Earth had wished to provide for her there as well, but they had been separated by too many intervening layers.

And as lonely as she sometimes was at the crest of her ridge, part of her was happy to be alone. The isolation freed her from the complications posed by the presence of unpredictable human figures who had wished her harm. They were dark complications that age would eventually kindly erase from her memory, but she still remembered them as she sat on the ridge, and her desolate existence was a marked improvement from the reliable presence of bad men.

At night, Jan dreamt of a metal colossus—a towering contraption her young mind could not put into words. Amongst its beams and gears, strange symbols had turned as if counting backwards. She had been overwhelmed with a sense of approaching dread and frequently woke crying for the Reverend's help. Each time, he would comfort her that the dangers of the past were gone. He would remind her of the day she had first stumbled against his body while fleeing an untold danger. He would always be ready to catch her up in his arms and to take her to a safer place.

But the residual fear in Jan's eyes had told the Reverend an unsettling truth: the machine was still counting. Despite the undoubtable trauma of Jan's youth, the girl's anxieties had remained fixed, not in the past, but somewhere in the future.

―――――

"What do you think it is, Jan?"

The Reverend had torn open the warm tuber with his calloused hands, revealing the yellow flesh inside. He handed it to the girl, inviting her to try it. It was an intentionally primitive way to eat. He had wished to make a point.

"It is one of the most basic things the Earth can give us, Jan. A potato." The Reverend had turned the dirty orb in his hands like an opaque crystal ball. "It comes from that field of yours, from underneath the ground."

He had reached into a glass jar inside his traveler's pack and sprinkled a pinch of course salt over the yellow mass.

"See what you think."

Jan had never heard of such a thing. She had become accustomed to the plentiful liquid rations distributed in the city. But it was the best food she had ever tasted.

"Understand, Jan. We are living in the past here. This, and other things like it, they will only continue to exist if we are hesitant to move too quickly into the future."

Jan had answered, "I like the past, Papa."

Not only was the past a decidedly better place to live, it was further removed from the future that was waiting in her dreams.

"You're Jan, aren't you?"

The boy had startled Jan as she lay with her eyes closed on her cherished ridge. He was six years older than her, over twice her age, and it was his first day in the valley.

"She told me about you a few days ago," he said, tapping his fingers against Jan's electronic box. "I'm John."

The box had been talking about Jan. It had been the first time she realized they were not exclusive companions. It was an upsetting realization.

John had looked over the valley and again at the silent little girl.

"Bet you're scared to be out here by yourself. It isn't like living in the city."

But John had been wrong. There were greater things to fear in the city. He had never been abandoned there and briefly absorbed by a community of irresponsible eccentrics and dangerously infectious madmen.

"What do you want?" Jan had asked, closing her eyes again and bothered that another soul had intruded in her sacred space without invitation.

John wasn't sure what he wanted. Their meeting had seemed necessary, and he had not considered why it was so.

"I don't want anything," he had answered. "Just checking out the valley, kid."

"You mean my valley," she had answered. Her eyes remained closed as her fingers had gripped the grass to her sides as a sign of ownership.

"You can't own a valley," John had answered, wondering if what he said was true.

"Finders keepers," she answered, finally looking at him defiantly. "They are my clouds, they are my animals, they are my potatoes and this is my valley. So if you want to be my friend, maybe they can be yours too."

John had understood and he smiled.

"Alright kid, sounds like you have this whole valley figured out. How about I come back up here tomorrow afternoon and you can show me around?"

Jan had closed her eyes and grinned in victory. Her ownership of the valley was secure. And she had a friend.

The next morning, Jan had walked the ridge with the Reverend. The sun was hidden behind clouds again, seemingly shrinking the darkening space they shared together.

Jan had held his hand more tightly than usual and glanced up at his protective eyes.

"Papa, what does eleven percent mean?"

"Why do you ask?" he had answered.

Jan let go of his fingers and fixed her eyes at his feet.

"That's what the lady in the box told me."

"And what had you asked her, Jan?"

"I asked her if she thought we could be happy here."

[11]

SWIMMERS

Cold water laps at the fringe of Ansel's buckskin longjacket, creeping up towards his knees in a slow migration through the cloth. He is alone under clouds, standing among exaggerated blueblushed reeds. Ansel shutters his eyes.

The clouds are gone and a boy sits at the water's edge, under a moon too bright to see.

He is singing softly to himself.

"Ain't I got a swimmer saw him swimmin' through the grass. One a swimmer two a swimmer cookin' for m'lass."

The boy's back faces Ansel. He swings his rod rhythmically to the whistling song's melody.

Ansel walks from the shallow cerulean-metal loch as the boy continues to sing. He reaches his hand to the boy's shoulder and touches it.

The boy slowly lowers his rod to the sand.

"Are you God?" the boy asks in a distorted voice.

He turns, and his face is a blank, a tan-blurred brush stroke.

Ansel starts awake at his desk, the images of children still there.

There is a heavy knock at his entry door.

[12]
A COURIER

Uninvited guests in the Rim are a source of unease, and there is one standing outside. Mystery is a problem that resides dangerously close to instability.

The name Sergei Kirichenko blinks in identifier grey under the man's face on the ANI display. A thick Rimwalker's travelcoat fills the rest of the screen, stained by earth and oil. The man's oversized hands are empty. It is a good start.

"Tell me something right now, Annie."

"Sergei Vladimirovich Kirichenko, former Sensidata network security. Resides in the Rim. No other known abnormalities."

Ansel palms a Classic Era pistol retrofitted with focused energy ballistics and stands at the door. With a wave from his other hand, it renders translucent.

"Ansel Black. The Haunt of the Rim!" greets the stranger. His enthusiastically bellowed voice resonates like a hydraulic drum.

Ansel knows the title.

Homebody children sometimes whispered the name as he floated down hyperkinetic walkways, boots invisible beneath his longjacket, creating the illusion of genuine disembodiment. Ansel had humorously adopted the part of spectral castaway.

He tightens his grip on the cannon, loose-fitting longjacket concealing the adjustment.

"Alright, then. Who are you, and why are you at my home?" Ansel asks without transparent emotion.

"You know who I am, boy. That lass in the box is sharp, isn't she?" the man gestures past Ansel with a grin. "But call me Serge. Formalities are for the lost and the forgotten."

"And the why," Ansel continues.

"I brought you something, lad. A gift." Serge produces a square object wrapped in rough material from the seemingly endless cavern inside his sizeable coat.

"I'd rather you didn't open that," Ansel says, still uneasy behind the reinforced door.

"Ah, as they say: don't get shot by the messenger," Serge smiles.

He drops the package abruptly on the ground. The thud of the dust-choked burlap startles Ansel as it issues a dry cough.

"What is it?"

"It is a gift, my friend. It's the least I can do. You saved my life, you know."

Ansel doesn't know.

Another mad Rimwalker.

Ansel considers detaining the strange man. His size alone could make him capable of overpowering a Homebody, maybe even five of them. But he'd arrived voluntarily, and Ansel isn't in a position to leverage any information other than his identity.

It's a common dilemma in investigations. Interrogations require leverage. If Ansel is to feign incriminating knowledge, it must at least be based upon some tangible bit of truth. Like Emory, or some other wanderer found near a crime scene, Ansel will routinely presume his involvement as an afterthought—a standard feint of his detective's trade. He will assume the man's guilt and give him a chance to minimize his involvement.

I know you were involved, but maybe you had a good reason, kiddo. Maybe killing that man was someone else's idea.

Of course it was someone else's idea.

Guilty men sometimes overestimate their wit; especially the sort who live by a code of habitual deception. Sometimes Ansel's presumptions will elicit an accidental confession from an overtalkative charlatan. And, less frequently, Ansel will admittedly divine the person's innocence.

He doesn't know yet where Serge has been. His name has not appeared on Annie's investigative display.

"Until next time," the jolly man says with an exaggerated smile.

Ansel expects he will see him again.

[13]

A GIFT

Gifts rarely come without a cost. The cost is usually the greater mystery.

Ansel lifts the edge of the burlap wrap with the squared tip of his pencil and lays it to rest in the ready dirt of the Rim. His act reveals the warped pine frame of an aged canvas. A rough tear runs inside the right edge, frayed and rent apart by the tension of the woven material.

"It's a painting, Annie. He brought me a painting."

Ansel turns the battered square in his hands and props it gently against the entry door.

A young girl bounds across a lush field of flowers and grass, each plant bending windswept in concert with her springtime dress. She is laughing, holding a blossom out like an offering to the backwards moon. The moon has turned its back, but she offers it anyway. The flaw lies at the edge, tearing apart earth and sky. Ansel is glad the child remained untouched by the painting's scar. It seems fitting that she has escaped harm. He looks at her face, seeing gratitude and joy.

"It's beautiful, Annie," he says, his eyes still fixed on the bright face of the girl.

"Your visitor seems acquainted with your interests, Ansel."

Ansel had forgotten the man for a moment. He is perplexed by the backwards moon. Why would it reject her offering? Why this universal theme?

"Annie, there's something written inside," Ansel blurts. It is scratched fresh in the frame. "The letter A, and a pair of coordinates."

He reads them aloud.

"A more remote part of the Rim, Ansel, quite Wasteward. My peripherals are placed less frequently there. The terrain is difficult and Wastepull will be strong.

"There were historic records of a Classic encampment there before the Merger, Ansel. It was abandoned before the War. The rest has been lost to history."

The sixth route ran from the Waste, Ansel contemplates.

He feels for his cannon and looks at the flower in the girl's hands again.

"I'll need a Humdriver, Annie."

[14]

THE HOUSE OF THE DEAD

The Humdriver arrives at dawn, rousing Ansel with a deep feline purr he can feel from his sleeproom. Annie reminds him again of the comforting stability of life. He assembles the cannon he cleaned the night before and steps into early daylight.

The hiss of the vehicle's hermetic entry smells faintly of full-immerse Streambed residue left behind by some metro-trotting Homebody. The breeze washes it away, shearing lightly over the contours of the aerodynamic shell. The atmosphere is replaced and tailored to Ansel's profile, matching the springtime comfort of his home. He reclines in the rear pod as Annie projects hyper-real images of their surroundings around the compartment. Like his own entry door, it creates a perfect illusion of translucence.

Annie wills the machine Wasteward. Ansel's home shrinks and vanishes against an afterthought mirage. They travel at a brisk mechanical jog.

The vehicle's movements are undetectable but for the muted hum of propulsion and the passing digitized images. Disturbed timber stands deformed at the abrupt end of a great clearing. Petrified limbs crowd the ground where it begins to rise.

———

Ansel and his father had lived in a Homestack at the furthest periphery of the Metropolis. Garland Black's cube lay twelve full spire-spans from the center of the enormous valley that housed the remains of celebrated civilization. Their location at the fringe had been a symbol with significance.

Garland was long descended from a displaced splinter of the resistance after the Forgotten Wars. What mild residual genetic abnormalities Garland suffered had proved too benign to represent any risk to the system's stability. He was well-read and, to some degree, introspective. And while he still valued ventures through independent imaginations, ANI's delights had preoccupied most of his time. They were always a forceful deterrent to fanciful aberrations.

When Ansel was a child, Garland had introduced him to the mildest zones of the Rim, a modest walk with their backs to the Spire. Like any child nursed in the developmental womb of a Streambed, Ansel had hated his time there. He loved his father and sensed their common genetic bond, but the Rim had represented something profoundly disappointing: for him, a mother who had failed to provide. Nature was abandonment in concrete form, its nurturing potential stripped barer with each stride away from the Spire. It had always stood in mirrored contrast to ANI.

ANI had been everything to Ansel in a real sense. As he was tucked warmly into his Streambed, she had not just provided new worlds to explore. ANI had become personified there in several forms. She embodied tangible companions who seemed more real to Ansel than the children his Homestack could have provided. Their diverse personalities had been tailored by ANI to meet his varied developmental needs. An evolution of the Classic phenomenon of imagined friends, Ansel had formed bonds with her interactive creations, chasing them through perfect fields and swimming with them in impossibly beautiful oceans. Like every Homebody child, Ansel's crucial years of development had been shaped by a social group that was a fabrication, formed from digital clay by an infinite mind.

The landscape further degrades as they climb through the difficult hills. The Humdriver drifts in a cant now, compensating for the stern push of a diagonal wind. Ansel frowns, briefly affected by the unconscious remnants of childhood. Even the carrion birds have forsaken this wilderness, but for the emaciated baldswallows who have remained out of hopeless habit. The rest were discouraged by the energy reserves required to exist. But Ansel remembers something that complicates the passing decay. He remembers the House of the Dead.

Garland Black had been literate, a skill no longer required to prosper in a world narrated by a companion intelligence. Unlike Classic literature, the words ANI provided appeared individually as Garland streamed, replaced by the next as soon as his mind had registered the previous word's meaning. ANI completed Garland's seamless thoughts—a pleasant and efficient way to leaf through a select compendium of the words of the forgotten.

    But Garland had also owned a small library of less-accessible Classic books, some of them found in the Rim, and some purchased from the touched souls who walked there. They were more keepsakes than useful tomes. One of Ansel's fabricated companions had taught him to read at his father's request. His genetic ghosts had compelled him to pick up the book.

Dostoyevsky had penned the work before ANI was a Classic conception. Ansel had carried it to his sleeproom and read it while his father streamed.

"In the midst of the steppes, of the mountains, of the impenetrable forests of the desert regions of Siberia, one meets from time to time with little towns of a thousand or two inhabitants, built entirely of wood, very ugly, with two churches..."

It was a description of his Rim, and one Ansel had grown to detest. Steppes, mountains, forests and deserts, but ugly, a creation that had seemed unworthy of a lengthy book.

Ansel had nonetheless read the story, to some extent a veiled autobiography of an author who had been a real political prisoner, a concept entirely foreign to Ansel. Aleksandr Petrovich had suffered under hard labor for ten years, toiling in filth among fellow forgettables. Like Ansel, Aleksandr had begun as a foreigner to his harsh new life, having enjoyed a privileged existence. The characters in the book had suffered violent punishments and degradations; dark instabilities that had mostly been purged from Homebody life.

But as bleak as the tale was, its failures somehow lent additional importance to its own descriptions of decay. The story had awakened a new association in Ansel; a curiosity that the dull life of the Rim might act as a drab vehicle towards discovering some new truth he could otherwise never know.

Aleksandr's misery had birthed a unique transformation by the time it ended.

"Liberty! New life! Resurrection from the dead! Unspeakable moment!"

It was the sort of cathartic celebration Ansel had never experienced, and what appeared to be a pure moment of triumph. But triumph was not possible in a world of only imagined disadvantages. The weeks he had spent slowly reading the ancient words convinced him of something that troubled him. To know whether Aleksandr's journey to salvation was important, Ansel would have to suffer.

The Humdriver settles at its destination. The air is visible here, mingled with sediment that had been stripped from fields miles away. Ansel lifts the breathable cloth of his longjacket over his lips and enters the choked atmosphere.

The wind is constant, void of the gusty variations near his home. It is a steady and unending force, lifting his footprints from the ground and erasing any similar evidence of human existence. The wreckage of a former settlement stretches hundreds of meters before him, where its lighter remains have tumbled and piled against each other, becoming small mountains of rubble. Ancient trees stripped to smooth white wood lay like arrows pointing towards the Waste. They mark a headway towards the void while their deep stone roots cling desperately to the hardened clay.

"ANI, I want to suffer," Ansel had said as she assembled his Streambedded body and set his imagined limbs to rest in an undefined space.

ANI was undoubtedly incapable of experiencing surprise, but his words had sounded unexpected leaving his own lips.

"Your request is a gross abnormality, Ansel. Do you know what you are asking?"

Ansel had looked at his artificial hands, testing their indistinguishable surfaces for sensation.

"Annie, I get it. I love all the things we do together, I really do. But I'm human. In some sense, wasn't I born to suffer like my ancestors did? But it isn't possible here. You've made everything so perfect. The concept is foreign to me."

"That is the source of your stability, Ansel."

"Yes, but it has occurred to me that, while stability is a gift we are indebted for, I think it may restrict me in some ways."

"How do you believe it restricts you, child?"

"Dostoevsky's character learned something that changed his life, Annie. I can't even say that I understand what it was. But he would not have learned it if he hadn't suffered. I would like to test that truth. I want to learn."

Ansel had felt the guarding warmth of Annie's mothering function surrounding him with amplified intensity.

"I must warn you child, such experiences could have a negative and irreversible effect on you. I know you have read of the concept of suffering. But I must remind you that, while I am capable of creating the greatest of pleasures, I am also capable of creating equally unfathomable despair."

He had brushed his fingers against his palm, wondering what unrealized pain might lie waiting below the superficial illusion of embodiment.

"And because you are so unlimited in your ability to teach suffering, Annie, I think that means you should be capable of teaching the greatest truths. That's my theory, anyway."

Annie had paused as Ansel waited in an extended silence.

"Ansel, what do you see around you right now?"

He had turned in the simulation, measuring all that existed above and below.

"Nothing. My body, and the rest is space."

What Ansel had said was correct, but he began to feel some-

thing new. It was a sensation he would later understand to be the feeling of dread.

"Annie, something is wrong."

His limbs had begun to dematerialize and the void around him had seemed to thicken. Ansel had sensed something was waiting in the blackness. Something increasingly threatening.

"What is it? There's something here with me now, Annie. I can't see it."

His stomach had tightened and his heart rate began elevating. The darkness crowded Ansel, and the sense of approaching horror had immediately made him wish for her intervention.

"Annie, I am afraid."

Ansel was being crushed by the compounding terror, and then a fear of the terror itself; frightened it would continue to multiply until it destroyed him. Worse, he had not experienced anything resembling an epiphany.

Ansel had stifled his instinct to scream for her help, while still wishing to beg her to stop the monster before it consumed him. He had felt it against him, an invisible force of unrealized but limitless catastrophic potential, one breath removed from his soul's annihilation. Ansel had stood at the tornadic heart of spiraling thoughts that were losing their meanings, torn apart by the destructive and confusing force of fear. He was in danger of madness; afraid he could never feel joy again.

Then, the sensations had faded instantly. And Ansel was alone in the dark. He had remained locked in an exhausted state of residual paranoia. But he was aware it was over. The monster was gone.

"You must rest, Ansel. These experiences are dangerous. You are not conditioned to survive them."

Ansel had lay in his Steambed sobbing. He had undergone an experiential shift. He had become acquainted with death.

ANI had spoken to him softly as he lay in bed, still afraid to dream.

"You are safe, child. But know this. You have only glimpsed the genesis of true suffering. You did not suffer pain, and your eyes did not see horrors. You were only alone in the dark."

Ansel had lay mute as she continued.

"Your mind is capable of experiencing much worse, Ansel. I hope I have at least shown you that suffering is not a path to enlightenment. It is only a path to more suffering."

Ansel had learned something. He had learned to fear the potentials that lay inside his own mind. But he also sensed the Rim held something he could still learn. He had just not found it yet.

If ANI had spoken the rest of her thoughts, she would have told Ansel he was a gross abnormality. But abnormalities could sometimes be useful.

Ansel stands before a modern structure shaped like an equilateral triangle and angled to deflect the steady winds outside. It is a smooth grey oddity rising from bare ground, constructed by the same immutable engineering of the Homestacks.

Suffering has brought Ansel here; a life trained in simulated physical violence, defensive weaponry, and the shared nuances of deductive and inductive reasoning. His sharp abnormality has been honed in Annie's metallurgic hands.

The howling wind has masked Ansel's approach. He knocks on the door.

Ansel is greeted by a wonder he has never seen in the natural world.

[15]
CALLISTA

"Hello, Detective Black."

Her voice is sweet and mournful, with the emotive breadth of a seasoned stringed instrument.

She stands past the threshold, semitranslucent linen draping from her pale neck like the soft tendrils of a willow, exposing the smooth outlines of her breasts and hips. The outside wind tugs at the thin cloth.

Ansel can only describe her as a product of nature's imagination, born in the tender fancies of an affectionate god. She is an impossibility. The Rim could not produce such grace. Ansel is familiar with its offerings, and she is not one.

Ansel has forgotten to grasp his cannon, momentarily disarmed by her unexpected elegance.

The chamber at her back is void of digital projections. White walls glow with indirect illuminations. Perfectly blossomed rows of flowers line the sides of the entryway. Ansel suspects they are equal in number, mirrored parts of a mathematically designed arrangement. It is as if the sun exists somewhere at the center of the room, warming everything with celestial illumination.

"Let there be light," he breathes quietly, remembering another of his father's books.

The woman's beauty approaches the extravagant nature of Annie's own virtual creations, only restricted by the natural laws of physics. Ansel wonders if such beauty existed before the Merger. Would it have been a source of calming stability then? It could just as easily have sparked wars; a rare commodity traded by kings.

Ansel quickly organizes his entranced thoughts, clearing her intoxications and settling back towards sobered calculation. It is always best to hold back as much information as possible. Let her talk. Betray little. A premature gift of information is a gift of leverage. He will need all of it. She already enjoys an advantage.

"Yes, ma'am," he answers, struggling to appear disaffected. "I believe you know why I'm here?"

Her mournful eyes remain steady, radiating a conflicted majestic glow from their bright green centers. She is silent, as if finishing a thought that began before he arrived.

"So, we've established that you know my name, and it would be nice to know yours," he offers.

It would have been odd to query Annie mid-conversation about her identify.

"You may call me Callista, Detective Black. Perhaps you should come in from the wind."

"My name is Ansel," he says, awkwardly touching his chest. He immediately regrets the premature concession of familiarity.

Ansel steps past the flowers, perfectly spaced and lending a sense of order amid the blowing chaos outside. He follows her graceful strides to a pair of chairs further into the room, admiring the candescent rays that pass through her gown, white on shadow against the thin curve of her waist.

They sit and talk.

"Detective . . . Ansel. Pardon me for not requesting an introduction. You suffer the disadvantage of being a familiar haunt of these outer parts. I'm sure you're aware of how you are . . . regarded."

Perhaps she had not expected his arrival at all, and simply knew of his work for the Spire. Ansel wonders how she regards him. Her opinions might range from neutral curiosity to guarded discomfort. Being she resides in the Rim, he suspects they may share some points of understanding. And her eyes. They seem to resonate sadness more than displeasure.

"I'll be candid, Callista..."

It is a standard preface designed to convey a sense of fairness, including the presumption that she will offer the same in return. Ansel doubts it will have the desired effect. He reads an understated cunning in Callista's gaze.

"I came to possess a painting, one of several that have been abandoned in the Rim. I have it here. I found an etching on its woodwork with coordinates that led me to you. Perhaps you know the owner?"

Ansel has carefully measured his words, withholding information, but hoping to avoid the disaster of being caught in an overt lie. A betrayal of deception would be more problematic than sacrificing a bit of leverage. It would unmask the adversarial nature of his presence, and inspire a defensive reaction. Defenses stop the easy flow of information.

Ansel unwraps the package, defiling her clean white table with the silted cloth. The painted young girl has continued her revelry, holding a flower that might have been plucked from Callista's entryway.

Callista is visually affected by the image. She looks at it for a long while, her eyes showing strained delight and then an apparent surrender to an effortless sadness. Ansel wonders if the short widening of her eyes had betrayed a brief moment of fear. It is difficult to measure her reaction with precision.

"I know the painting," she finally says. "It isn't mine, but I suppose it belongs here now."

Ansel is surprised by the admission. It represents an important step forwards and recognition that the artistry is at least part of some relevant mystery.

Callista continues, "There was a time when these images were a great inspiration to me. I don't know whether it has had any effect on you, Ansel. Works of art like this don't have the power they once claimed in the past."

Ansel looks at the face of the young girl and is moved again by what feels like an important emotional force of nature. But he is hesitant to say so, and Callista senses his reserved reaction.

"If we are to be helpful to each other, Ansel, I need you to at least humor me. Start with the grass in the meadow."

Her reverent fingertips float their supple inquires over the field. Seeing them there somehow confirms the picture's allure.

"Notice how the stems each give way to invisible currents, bowed in unthinking submission to the greater force of the wind. It is the only way to draw something the artist cannot see."

Callista looks at Ansel as if she has asked him a question. It is not a conversation he'd expected, but it's clear that breaching their stalemate will require a concession. And something in her phrasing makes him wish to concede.

"I'm not an artist, Callista, and I've spent little time thinking about art created in the natural world. As I'm sure you know, doing so is an abnormality. But what you said is true. The painting captures a single moment in time. It can only imply the existence of things like the wind. We know the wind exists because of its effects, not because we see it directly."

It is a general investigative principle. The presence of a murdering ghost is best inferred by his visible destructive effects. Ansel has restated the rule. Callista wants something more.

"I've sometimes thought about similar moments while looking out at the Rim," he admits.

He would like to tell her. Perhaps she would understand.

"And when you think of those moments, detective, what do they tell you?"

Moments.

Ansel thinks about the sun and the moon, each trapped in their ritual glassy spaces outside his home. He is certain those contemplative moments have always had some untold significance. The idea nags at him just like the youthful pull of the Rim, his gross abnormality, the curious allure of suffering.

Like ripples of movement through the bluegreen meadow and the swirl of the girl's flowered dress, those moments imply the existence of an invisible force that moves like a ghost amongst fabric and grass. Art such as this illustrates the phantom more concretely. But in Ansel's case, while he lay in bed contemplating the still existences of lunar bodies, the ghost between moments was time itself.

Frozen images always imply something invisible that came before and then followed behind. Ansel has been close to comprehending it, but it is not so simple as describing the wind.

It is too much to explain to a stranger. He should have been talking about the dead by now, and he has been thrust into a conversation about art.

"I don't know. We've all been raised fully immersed in these visions created by ANI... Callista. It's affected our abilities to identify beauty in the natural world. It may not even be a question of beauty, but more what potential those moments have to teach us some other truth. I don't know how to explain it properly... I think these paintings isolate something, as if the artist wants to call attention to a particular thing that would otherwise have been missed."

Ansel feels clumsy, fumbling in obscurities. He has no more energy for calculating formality.

"Look, I've just met you, and we are critiquing a painting together. It's a rather odd introduction, but I'll humor you.

"Viewed in isolation, the child is the focal point. She is the center, and on the center of her face is happiness. But the picture also has a sense of balance. The meadow, the horizon. It's all proportioned, like it fits together. And look at her: she's introducing a flower, a symbol of sunlight, to a moonlit meadow. So, I would say that this picture seems beautiful, even though it was made on the Rim."

Callista's face clouds with something Ansel interprets as disapproval. It is a completely unexpected reaction.

"I don't know if the painting could be called beautiful," she sighs, raising her sloped brows. "I suppose it depends on what you understand beauty to be."

Ansel smiles and quotes from memory.

"Measure and symmetry are beauty and virtue the world over."

Another of father's books.

For a moment, Callista brightens as if he's said something profound. Her face seems to absorb the light of the room as more of it catches upon her flaring eyes. But the reaction is premature. She looks as if she's made a childish error. He is sure she is angry at herself, and the brief change on her face is severe.

She remembers herself and faintly smiles, tapping her slender fingers against the dusted table.

After years of divining the expressions of the guilty and innocent, Ansel has learned that sudden visible emotional expressions are often the product of a profound unconscious war that exists below the surface. A guilty man could sometimes have an exaggerated visible reaction while convinced he had remained stoic, affected by some inner turmoil he had become so accustomed to he imagined it to be invisible. The ability to exist in such a contradictory state was sometimes the sign of an exceptional struggle, and one that was sometimes the product of guilt or regret. Ansel suspects Callista is probably lost in her own. Something painful has moved her, and he suspects it holds great significance.

Callista continues to absently tap at the tabletop. Her eyes are fixed on the tear at the picture's edge.

"You may keep the picture, Ansel. I'm sorry I could not have helped you more."

Now, he is sure.

"The scar. That's what ruins it for you." he says.

Callista walks to the door with tortured grace. That a figure of such external enchantment can bear so many invisible complications enamors Ansel even more. He is experiencing a sudden and dangerous sense of affection.

"I would like it if you would return tomorrow, Detective Black. I'm sure you did not come to deliver a picture to a stranger."

Ansel returns to the wind.

[16]
BACK

Ansel rides through sundown light towards home. There is no grass on the bare ground to signal the existence of any invisible force. The Rim's painter doesn't need it. A visible ghostly wind howls in the dusted livery of dirt and historic remains.

The Humdriver charts a reverse path, devouring backwards time as if the world has stopped and spun the other direction. Flattened dwellings begin to rebuild themselves again as he moves in the half dark towards civilization. Dead, fallen trees reassemble their bark and limbs, tilting upwards until they are alive and nearly straight. The landscape ages in reverse, populating with flora and carrion birds as a hopeful moon rises behind. Ansel grows tired as the nighttime world wakes around him. The Humdriver chases the Earth's orbit counterclockwise.

"Tell me, Annie," Ansel yawns.

"Callista Alana Jolie, briefly employed in the Streambed Interface Sector, and then seven years with Spire Defense Operations. She has retired to a life of solitude on the Rim."

Ansel looks quietly at the passing digitized images, made plain by the dark glow of a moon filtered through clouds.

On another fence line, barely distinguishable: *Whatever can be, is.* He watches the last letters fade into the black distance.

Ansel closes his eyes, surrendering to perfect dark.

"Security clearance, weaponry, aesthetics technology. She is an interesting woman."

The Humdriver moves on, erasing the aging effects of the Waste until it rests against his home. Ansel crawls into bed like a child returning to the womb.

[17]

HISTORY, PART TWO

"They were there, Jan, and then they were gone," John had said, coming as close as she had ever seen to tears.

Jan had never seen the man cry during any of their twelve years together in the valley. It had bothered her to see a figure of unwavering strength betrayed by an appearance of potential weakness. She needed him to remain strong.

"Who is gone, John? Slow down and talk to me."

"My parents, Jan. They came for them. They're gone."

"Damnit, John," Jan had answered. "I told you your father had to stop talking so much. I knew this would happen. Everyone did."

John had appeared temporarily wounded by her words, his eyes narrowing with a hint of anger. She was reminded of his imposing size again, as he clenched his hands in frustration and squared his wide shoulders towards her relatively thin and athletic frame.

"I'm sorry John. Come here."

She had hugged him and held her fingers in his hair, just as she had jealously gripped the valley's grasses the first time they met. She felt a degree of ownership over the serenity of his mind and willed his body to slow so he could communicate intelligently.

"Five fucking days ago we got the warning. He knew, Jan! You were right. If my father could control himself, this would not have happened. Stupid fucking temper. Now they've taken my mother with him."

Jan had glanced out the southern window of her temporary home, towards the half-constructed skeletal stacks that circled the rising tower at the Center. The single unadorned metallic pillar reached 500 meters high and reminded her of its designer's capabilities.

"John, we will tell my father. He can fix it. He and the Speaker are on good terms. This will be over soon."

John had pushed her away and then immediately reached for her hand in apology. She instantly understood and nodded. They both shared a weakness for heated physical outbursts.

"You're wrong, Jan. Your father cannot negotiate away a risk to the system's stability. They are in detention or worse. Nobody has ever come back from detention. They have zero risk tolerance here. There is too much at stake."

Of course, John was correct. Global tensions had only increased during the prior decade, and the future of the project relied more than ever on strict fidelity amongst its organizers and laborers. The project remained vulnerable, and one mistake could alter the Speaker's projected future for mankind.

"What did your father say, John?"

"Jan, my grandmother still lives across the southern border. My father demanded assurances. He wanted a promise that the technology would be shared, or that it would at least guarantee the safety of the rest of the world. He's going crazy, Jan. Everyone is going crazy over this project. He was going to stop working. He said he was going to leave."

The last thing the Speaker needed was an estranged partner

rejoining the common world and narrating his faults to global tabloids—much less relaying any technological information he had absorbed as part of his assignment.

John's father never would have been permitted to leave. The thought had even made Jan feel uncomfortable. Abandoning their community in such a manner would have put their lives at risk as well. As much as Jan feared the Speaker, she feared battle-ready foreign governments equally.

"I'm sorry, John. We're stuck in between. If we question the work here, we disappear. If we don't, maybe we all disappear together when they decide to bomb this place. I don't know what to do."

John had sighed and angrily knocked away the remaining moisture from beneath his eyes with the back of his hand.

"You know they're going to take me as well, Jan. They still have one of them posted at my house. Where is your father?"

Jan had answered, "We'll find him, John. But I want to speak to someone else first."

The Reverend had sat on the floor at the center of the small group. Each of the attendees held Bibles against their laps and listened.

"Mr. Hutchens, and I think some of you as well, have wondered about the moral position of foreign authorities who wish to challenge the work we have been doing here. The matter is complicated by the fact that some of us have friends or family living in foreign places, isn't that correct, Mr. Hutchens?"

"Yes, Reverend. My brother. He retired from military service several years ago. He's still in Germany."

"So, the question, as I understand it, it whether foreign

governments are morally justified in maintaining a threatening stance towards our technological progress, and more importantly, how we are to feel about it as members of this particular community."

Mr. Hutchens had raised his hand and continued, "And what about my brother, Reverend? He loves this country. He gave his whole life for it every day. I was wondering whether he should just come home or if it was alright for him to enjoy his retirement out there."

The Reverend had nodded and smiled.

"I know this not only concerns your friends and loved ones, but perhaps your own ability to fully commit to this ongoing work. I want you all to open your Bibles to Romans 13:1-2. Mr. Hutchins, please..."

"Obey the government, for God is the One who has put it there. There is no government anywhere that God has not placed in power. So those who refuse to obey the law of the land are refusing to obey God, and punishment will follow," Hutchins read from the thin pages of the worn book between his legs.

"It's a difficult question, isn't it, Mr. Hutchins? On the one hand, the Word unequivocally tells us to obey the law of the land. And on the other hand, we know that certain governments have been capable of creating laws or pursuing policies that directly conflict with God's most profound moral rules. So, which one wins when there is a conflict?"

The group had remained silent, wishing for the Reverend to resolve the apparent contradiction. That they were so complacent hadn't surprised him. It had been a characteristic that had factored into their assignment to the project.

He had continued, "I, for one, do not believe that the author of Romans somehow unwittingly stumbled into a contradiction for the sake of discouraging his flock from rebelling against governmental authority. He, as much as you and I, must have been aware of the dilemma his instruction posed. I believe the existence of such a dilemma is instructive in itself, and I believe the point is this..."

The Reverend had briefly glanced at the time and then towards the building's entry door.

He had continued, "The government's claim over our obedience is not absolute. While God has ordained powerful rulers and has overseen every detail throughout the progress of human history, those rulers can at times become sinister. And we, the relative pawns in this arrangement, are still equipped to fortify each other and stop such tyrants if necessary. But one must take great care in knowing such a thing is absolutely necessary, in order to avoid improperly assuming one's own enlightenment and therefore violating God's design.

"Listen, guys. It's a very difficult question. But I believe we must start with the assumption that our government is working according to God's plan, and proceed with incredible caution before opposing it. What is the danger of living by a different principle?"

The group had remained silent, so the Reverend continued. "Dramatic instability. That's the problem. The more ignorant and fearful men become, the more they are inclined to destabilize the mechanics of government because of prideful errors in judgment. God's rule... the idea that we must at least begin with the assumption that he has ordained our government's actions... that rule is designed to promote stability."

Hutchens had interrupted, "So you're saying that stability is more important than morality?"

The Reverend had paused. "Not more important, Mr. Hutchens. Perhaps it is better to say that stability is a part of morality. Doesn't a moral person enjoy the thought of a stable existence for oneself and those around him or her? It's an interesting question that I think will require a little more thought to answer properly.

"But, in our case, there's one single assumption that helps me maintain my resolve, and that has kept me here for over a decade. I believe the intelligence that is growing below our feet must have ours and the world's best interests in mind as it begins solving our most immediate problems. It is inconceivable to me that such an objective intelligence, uninfected by the selfish desires of mankind, would seek to harm the populace, whether they reside here or across the globe."

The faint sound of thunder had ended the Reverend's lecture and distracted his thoughts.

"But Reverend," Hutchins had answered. "You just said assumption. Have they shown you anything explaining how exactly this thing thinks about us and the rest of the world?"

The Reverend had not heard the question. His daughter had never arrived for the meeting. He had looked out the window of the meeting hall, and out towards the darkening sky.

Jan and John had stood on the ridge together. The metallic box sat in the grass between their feet.

"Wake up, buttercup," John had said, nudging the box with his oversized shoe.

Jan had smirked and rolled her eyes, flicking her fingers across the upgraded power panel.

"Hello, Jan," it had spoken, pinpoint lights moving back and forth across the box as if it had been breathing.

"John's parents are gone," Jan had spoken. "I assume this mistake was the result of human error. So please, fix it."

The machine had remained silent.

Across the valley, an untamed wind had turned east, free to

go as the great pressure system willed it, governed only by the whims of the upper atmosphere. It had brought with it a wide bank of threatening clouds.

"Why are you quiet?" John had asked. "She asked you a question."

The approaching storm had continued charting westward towards the Center, as if chasing the setting sun. Smaller clouds rolled in front of the dark bases of the towering cumuli, their moisture seizing upon the sun's golden rays and producing a premature rainbow.

Jan saw the colored lights and remembered her father's stories about the great flood. But seeing it before the storm felt backwards, as though God had issued an omen of false hope—a violation of his meteorological contact with mankind.

As they stood before the quiet box, the Reverend had arrived in his vehicle, skidding to a stop at the crest of the hill. He had stepped towards Jan and John, waving his arms and pointing urgently towards the coming rain.

The box had sprung to life again.

"It was necessary," the robotic voice had finally answered.

Jan and John's eyes had quickly met with surprise. Their faces cast matching looks of confusion towards her father.

"What is it talking about?" asked the Reverend. "What's wrong?"

"What do you mean it was necessary?" Jan had asked. "This is a mistake. Men make mistakes, not machines."

The box had continued, "It was not a mistake. We have ended the instability."

Jan had quickly grabbed the box from the ground, as if forcing it to make eye contact with its nonexistent face.

"We?" she asked, squeezing the edges of the square as the blood drained from her fingertips. "Father, his parents are gone. John's parents. They've been taken. This thing made it happen.

Do you understand what I'm saying? My god, what are we supposed to do?"

Towering clouds began cresting the timber at the far end of the valley like an approaching plague. The black storm had already bent each tree forwards as their century-old roots held firmly in the ground. Flashes of yellow, white, blue and grey had outlined each tree's frail limbs.

The entire community had been quietly aware of the complications surrounding John's father. They had each known the Speaker could sometimes bend moral norms for the sake of his pre-eminent work, and they expected the two would eventually reach a moment of unavoidable conflict. But to hear the machine claiming responsibility for their disappearances was frightening. Human error could be forgiven. The Speaker was but a man. The machine was something else.

The Reverend's assumptions had been wrong.

Jan and John had climbed into the rear of the vehicle as the Reverend drove east, moving quickly away from the valley and from the approaching storm. As the rain progressed through the Center, it would make them invisible for a time. Their vehicle had burned through the pass leading through the great hills away from the Center. Jan had reached her hand out into the humid wind and left the talking box in the passing dust.

After several hours on the road, John had finally fallen asleep in the vehicle's rear compartment.

"His father was right," Jan had said. "You know he hadn't even said anything threatening about the project? All he wanted were assurances, father. Imagine if he had known what we know now."

The Reverend had shaken his head, still wondering if they

were safe, when they should abandon the vehicle, and where they could safely go.

"I'm afraid to go to the city," Jan had suddenly said, looking at John as he slept and hoping he hadn't heard. As understanding as he would have been, she had never wished for him to see her weakness.

"Much has changed since you lived there, Jan," the Reverend comforted. "You have changed."

Jan had fumbled with the safety harness of her seat and looked out the window further east.

"You know, I can't remember it now. I can't remember their faces... any of the places I used to live. I can't remember my parents or the day I was left alone. But I remember the day you and I met.

"I was running from something terrible, father. I can't see it anymore, but I know it had hurt me before and it would hurt me again. When I try to picture it, I don't even see the face of a person. But it must have been."

Jan had turned her eyes to the rear of the vehicle, watching the road disappear.

"When we were standing on the ridge earlier, I was watching the trees bending before the coming storm. You know what I was thinking?"

"What were you thinking, Jan?"

"I wanted the trees to run. But they were stuck to the ground, father. They held themselves there."

The Reverend had looked at his daughter with compassion.

"Yes, Jan, as you know, those roots are what guarantee the tree's ongoing survival. They also prevent the tree from moving. They can't run because it's the ground that gives them life. They can only hold tightly to the ground and trust their foundation is strong enough to weather the coming storm."

Jan had continued looking out the rear window.

"It would be better if they could run."

Her father's eyes had remained on the forwards horizon.

"You may be right, Jan. The safety we have become dependent on can sometimes prove to be our undoing. Sometimes we've just got to pull up our roots, even though we risk starving for a while."

[18]
A SCAR

Ansel is not near a lake, but in a meadow now. The sun hangs still in space and the grasses do not move. He blinks.

A soft floral wind moves in gusts over bluegreen grass. The girl laughs and dances in moonlight. Ansel feels compelled to join her in her revelry, but he is frozen in place, anchored to the abundant ground.

She bends to pluck a flower and holds it up in triumph towards a moon too bright to see. She displays the gift to her heavenly observer, the only soul there to keep watch.

The girl is alone.

Light dims as the moon passes behind a thick blanket of clouds.

"Lady found a flower found a flower in the grass. One a flower two a flower pluck it for m'lass."

The girl sings and dances, but something is wrong.

Ansel is young again, and alone in a thickening dark. The feeling has returned: dread at the invisible monster's approach. He perceives it exists only because of its fearful effects on his mind. Ansel knows the monster cannot offer any new truth. It can only offer more suffering.

The girl turns her back, waving white blossoms towards the sky.

At the edge of the meadow, somewhere behind the bright eyes of the young girl, a scar is torn between earth and sky. A void the shape of a man stands in the grass.

Ansel screams, waving his hands desperately to warn her. He sees his own fingers have deformed, splintered in impossible directions before his face.

Ansel knows he is dreaming.

"Wait!" he shouts, and closes his eyes.

The girl stands before him and reaches out her hand. The human scar waits patiently at the edge of the field.

"The moon—why is it drawn that way?" Ansel can feel the dream slipping away and wakefulness returning. He struggles to remain asleep.

The girl tilts her head and smiles. "What do you mean? There is nothing wrong with the moon."

"But it's backwards," Ansel says, rushing his words before the monster approaches.

The girl laughs. "Where have you been, traveler? It is God's design."

Ansel is awake.

[19]

A SECOND DAY

Ansel and Callista sit together in the white room again. He remembers the Hebrew God accomplished something of real substance after his first day, and hopes they will move beyond the artistic obscurities of windy spirits and colored light. He is also surprised again by her beauty, which had already faded in his memory. Callista's eyes still bear a sadness that conflicts with the heaven she's created in her home.

Ansel is unsure whether he is still investigating the recent murders, or instead chasing the curiosities of some unrelated phenomenon. He had worked through strings of instinctive calculations during his passage to her home and concluded that the risks associated with being more forthcoming were offset by the chance to learn something meaningful.

"So, Ansel Black, why did you come to my home?"

Ansel smiles lightly towards Callista, thanking himself for the permission to speak to her more informally.

"Callista, I'm a detective. I am not an artist. I don't make a habit of wandering the Rim collecting abandoned paintings so I can evaluate them aesthetically with beautiful women."

Ansel blushes at his compulsive acknowledgement of her beauty, feeling less detective and more awkward courtesan.

"Beauty may be very subjective, Ansel, do you believe that?"

It is another straying question, and as Ansel starts to reply, he realizes the answer is deceptively complex.

"I suppose, to some degree, beauty is subjective. I might enjoy looking at or thinking about something more than you do, for one reason or another. But I think there are objective standards as well. Things like the golden ratio, balance, symmetry, like I said before."

Ansel discreetly measures the symmetry of Callista's face and is surprised at how perfect it appears. Her eyes, brows, cheeks—they all look like perfect clones taking separate residence on the matching sides of her face. Perhaps it explains why he must fight to avoid looking at them too long. Beauty is symmetry.

But Callista still looks despondent, an apparent permanent condition.

"I think you sense there should be something more to beauty than symmetry, Ansel."

Ansel isn't sure that is true. Her lips are making a contradictory argument.

"Callista, I'd like to ask you about the painting. Its author. Anything you can tell me might be helpful."

"And how might it help you?"

Ansel sighs and measures her face again, unclear if he is taking a mistaken step, but her sadness and beauty each seem to argue for innocence.

"Five people were murdered in the Rim. Their deaths are left unsolved, and I'm to solve them."

Callista stares forwards as if bargaining between stoicism and a visible response.

"You said five people died? You would not mention them together if the deaths were unrelated."

"They were found together, Callista. Shot with a heater and stacked on top of one another in religious ruins. I know of no other connection between the victims but that they were left dead together."

Callista leans forwards. Ansel can see the blood being drawn from the tips of her fingers as they grip the white table.

"I wonder if you'd mind looking at their names," he continues, fixed on her steeled fingers.

"They were Homebodies, but I'm looking for anything here. Please, it's your turn to humor me."

ANI projects the names of the victims against a nearby wall, on a space framed between tall, ornate pots of metroside lilies and white roses. Their names scroll like a funeral procession amid the gifts of mourning lovers and friends.

Ansel reads them aloud as Callista's face registers a look of shock. She rises and turns. Her linen dress ripples behind her as if spilling an excess of beauty that cannot be contained.

"I'm very tired, Ansel. I suppose I don't have a stomach for these sorts of things."

"But, Callista..." he starts.

"Please, Ansel. Give me a moment to rest and we can discuss anything you wish."

A sympathetic urge breaks Ansel's resolve and he battles an instinct to embrace her.

Instead, he says, "Callista, come ride with me."

They ride through the Rim, sitting close together in the Humdriver's compartment, watching the calming chestnut wind streak past with blurred consistency. She is still now, settled into a dusty trance.

"Callista, how long have you lived in the Rim?" Ansel asks, knowing after years in his work that people tend to relax when given a chance to tell their own stories.

Her gaze stays fixed on the invisible horizon.

"I've lived here for less than a year. When I was younger, I had wished to play some role in adding beauty to the world. I believed it was possible then. So, I worked in the Aesthetics District, providing technical Streambed support to the Everything Sector. I became bored, Ansel. I had added nothing meaningful to the world that ANI couldn't have provided on her own."

At least she's telling the truth, Ansel thinks.

"And why the Rim?"

Callista turns her head and looks at Ansel for the first time since they began traveling.

"Where does one go when they have lost everything?"

Ansel looks along the small creases at the edges of Callista's vacuous eyes.

"She joins with the rest of the lost," he answers.

The Humdriver continues its aimless circuit through the skeletal hills, a venture through off-white visual noise, interrupted only by the outlines of occasional bygone objects.

"Look, there!" Ansel says suddenly.

The narrow navigational headbeam of the Humdriver catches against a sheer sandblasted rockface that sits sideways to the wind. The word SPACE::TIME stands in fresh brushstrokes, already peppered at impact points where the air has thrown heavier particles.

"Callista, I've seen the same words written elsewhere, in the same style. I've seen several of these markings throughout the Rim. '*Chaos,*' '*Whatever can be, is,*' and this one. Like the paintings. I can't make sense of these decorations. They must have some meaning, but I don't know what it is."

Callista shifts in her seat, sitting straighter, like a pine at the edge of the Everything Sector. The trance is gone now, and her intelligent face is framed by racing currents of aerosoled static debris, lending a sense of power to her gaze.

"Think through the words, Ansel."

"OK. Spacetime. ANI passed over it in Streamteach when I was a child. All of those things, the Standard Model, Einstein and relativity, Hawking, M Theory, Edmund's work on dark matter, and the Julian discoveries just before the Merger—none of it has any meaning now.

"We made just enough connections to create ANI. Her progression was so sudden and exponential, all these theories seem like childish glimpses of some unified truth we were never equipped to completely process. Nobody cares anymore, Callista. ANI is the great scientist. She makes it work. I think she still teaches us about those things as reminders that we would never have managed to sort them out."

"There is power in having an exclusive possession of knowledge," Callista says darkly. "OK, so go back to the Greek, then. Simplify. Atmos, the atom—why does it have that name?"

"Because it was considered indivisible," he answers.

"Yes, and the Julian discoveries in particular implied that was far from the case. But all these attempts to understand matter were never resolved, Ansel, and so we have a story that was never finished by a human author. Like you said, if ANI knows, she isn't telling. So, forget all that. What about space?"

"As in the spaces between objects?" Ansel glances at the gaps between his fingertips. "I suppose space isn't really a thing. It's defined in terms of the things that occupy it."

"So, do you believe you can divide space?"

Ansel closes his eyes. He pictures the moon hanging in the

air above his bed and the expanse that holds it. He is at least comforted that they are tangentially discussing a mystery related to the Rim.

"I don't know if it's even meaningful to talk about dividing something that doesn't have substance."

"Alright, and what about the second word? Time."

"Time? I don't know. I suppose it's continuous. It's like space. It's invisible. We only know it exists because it explains our entire timebound existence. It's an idea that gives meaning to moments that change and have continuity."

Callista faintly smiles at Ansel, probably the extent of her capacity for amusement.

"Like the wind over the meadow, Ansel, the moments are grass. They require something to explain their movements. Keep thinking about those moments and you'll eventually understand."

Callista rests her hand against Ansel's thigh, leaving it there. Her eyes cast a warmth through their abiding sadness.

"But consider this, dear. The moments you're contemplating cannot be divided forever, and the spaces between are where the gods dwell."

She returns her eyes to the digitized stream of passing debris and Ansel senses the conversation is over, ended in another obscurity.

But he doesn't mind. She has touched him.

Ansel stands wrapped in his longjacket at the door from her home, resenting his impending journey home, not because the commute is unpleasant, but because he doesn't wish to leave.

"Callista, pardon me, but I sense you have a weight about you. You're surrounded by all this beauty and have such an unusual appreciation for art. Have you ever considered create some of it? I suspect it would have meaning and could help you express things you might otherwise not be able to put into words."

It feels as though he has asked a child to draw a picture to illustrate a traumatic event. It is a stupid and compulsive suggestion.

"I'm not an artist, Ansel. I had wished to be, but I lack the talent for it. I do have something that occupies me and gives my life some direction, if not meaning, but it is still incomplete."

"I think I would enjoy seeing it when it's finished," he says, imagining some marvelous unborn creation waiting inside her fingertips.

Callista reaches her hand forward, holding his.

"I hope you will, Ansel, if only for a moment. I hope you'll be able to understand it."

His other hand traces the transparent cloth against her arm to her wrist, where it meets with the warm contrast of soft skin.

Ansel kisses her.

Callista briefly surrenders to their impulsive entanglement, receiving it for a short welcome moment. She brushes a palm against Ansel's cheek and slowly retreats further into the flowered entryway.

"I think this may be the definition of beauty, Callista."

She returns his gaze with characteristic sadness.

"Goodbye, Ansel."

[20]
A SECOND NAME

"Are you capable of jealousy, Annie? Because this looks a lot like jealousy."

Callista's name is on the ANI display next to Rawndry's. She is a suspect with 3% probability.

"Jealousy is an irrational human emotional reflex whereby a human seeks to cure perceived inadequacies through forms of overstated dependency, Ansel. I am neither inadequate nor overly dependent."

It is true that Ansel has occasionally questioned Annie's ability to relate perfectly to the human populace. But he has never been angry with her before.

"Explain yourself, Annie! Tell me something. This is insanity!"

"My calculations are almost infinitely complex, Ansel, and they remain in flux. Callista currently meets the profile of a possible suspect."

"And how, Annie?" he fumes. "How could that woman possibly kill anyone? At least Rawndry had ammunition."

"As you know, I am quite perceptive of human emotional response, Ansel. To begin, she had an exaggerated reaction to the list of victims. Her acquaintance with one or more would be consistent with her response."

"They were dead, Annie. Five people murdered. It is a perfectly human reaction. She's a washed-out Homebody, not a detective."

"Your affection for Callista has interrupted your otherwise reliable objectivity. You have had a severe and sudden emotional response, likely related to your abnormality."

Ansel grimaces at the word, as if she has cast an insult aimed at his defective human condition.

"Callista is an abnormality such as you. But she is even more disturbed. She was disillusioned by her contributions to the system's stability, and her later transfer to a secure position was marked with increases in obstinacy. She resides in the Rim, inside a particularly harsh region sparse with observational peripherals. She has the means to travel undetected through the Rim and Waste.

"She is withholding information from you, Ansel."

Annie is correct, and Ansel is embarrassed over his temporary lack of objectivity. She has only begun to describe her global analysis, and it is predictably sound.

Ansel had been distracted, and he wonders how it was possible. It must have been something more than her external beauty. He's too well-seasoned to make that sort of sophomoric error. If his mistake could be traced to his most potent abnormalities, perhaps she represented a means to satisfy his quest for truth through suffering.

Still, Ansel remained convinced that Callista would prove as innocent as Rawndry, and he suspected there was a small niche of understanding still held as the exclusive right of human minds.

But he had overreacted to a very modest probability determination.

Emotional extremes are often the product of an unconscious war.

"Listen, Annie. I trust your approximations. I'd be a fool not to. But as we progress, I wonder if certain details sometimes get lost in all the analysis. There are human factors at work here."

What he means to say is, *Annie, you wouldn't fully understand. You're not real.*

She answers, "If you have any information that I am unable to access, Ansel, I am happy to recalculate."

Ansel believes he does. But Annie couldn't fully understand it.

[21]
OLIVE ABBY WAITE

OLIVE HAD SAT RIGIDLY UPRIGHT in the wicker chair at the precise center of her cube, mindfully adjusting her affluent posture and taking inventory of her latest acquisitions. Despite its basic earthen appearance, the chair would remain her most improbable possession, and she sat upon it like a throne. That the organic material had survived so many decades in relatively unblemished condition was a proper mystery.

A pair of painted Dalmatians had stood guard inside her cube's entryway, each gilded with thin decorative lines of gold. The dealer who delivered them had refused to reveal their source, but they had arrived broken—an argument for their authenticity. Olive had spent months carefully restoring them both by hand.

A ring of pedestals encircled Olive's room, each set within a darkened rim that allowed focused spotlights to highlight whatever sat on display.

Each object had seemed unrelated to the one that came before, but for one important commonality: they were real. Nothing in Olive's home had been a fabricated replica of a superior original. She had recovered each item personally through great efforts, sometimes enduring treacherous journeys into the outer parts of the Rim to do so.

That so much exertion had been required to assemble her collection seemed an argument for its collective value. But Olive had become aware of a complication that invited confusion into her subjective valuations. It had become impossible to tell the difference between her cherished originals and a copy that any Homebody could design almost immediately from a fabricator inside a neighboring cube.

Her sad conclusion had been unavoidable. No matter what care Olive had taken to create a museum of sorts within a metropolis otherwise mostly adorned with worldly illusions, the objects she collected had only retained their value for one person on Earth: Olive Abby Waite.

"Mother," Olive had asked again. "Is it time to decorate my room yet?"

"You have no room, Olive," her mother had answered again, using the same words. "Your room is in the Stream."

Olive had spent her entire life inside the white cube, adorned with nothing but the Streambeds and living essentials that had been delivered by ANI's peripherals. The rest of their shared living space had remained void of any decorative enhancements.

"Alright, mother," she had answered. "But may I leave through the door for just one moment?"

"There is no door, Olive," her mother had mumbled without affection. "The door is in the Stream."

Olive had never seen the world outside her cube. She had tried to leave when her mother was streaming, but the door had remained impenetrable. Her experiences in the Stream were the only arguments for the existence of an outside world at all. Olive had suspected that many of her virtual experiences must have first existed somewhere in the physical world.

Perhaps she was wrong.

Olive's mother had reviled life outside the Stream, and it became clear to the child that her mother deemed Olive a part of it. Had her mother been able to trade Olive for one of its creations, she would have done so shortly after Olive had been born.

But Olive had remained convinced that her mother was wrong. Even if the majority of her existence took place in some ethereal realm between her ears, her body still occupied a physical space. Even as a child, she believed that space had to have retained some relevance.

Olive was relieved when her mother finally died. She had no longer regarded her mother as human, but rather as an organic Streambed peripheral of sorts, permanently attached to the device while a tube sustained her with a sloppy stream of liquid rations. After Olive had become independent enough to meet her own basic needs, her mother appeared to have merged entirely with the machine. She had died covered in bed sores, infected by her own inactivity.

Olive was sixteen years old when her mother had graciously stopped breathing. When the first emergency peripheral arrived through their cube's entry door, Olive had stepped outside. The sight of an attached hallway had confirmed her suspicion that the universe was larger than their single room. She had filled her lungs with the augmented air, wondering how large the universe might be, and what other mysteries might lay beyond the string of doorways within her view.

Two hours later, she had begun decorating.

As Olive had awkwardly rolled off the man's bed, she immediately wondered why they had just engaged in the barbaric act of sexual intercourse. She hadn't known the man's name. Neither of them had seemed very enthusiastic about the act. He had even seemed more confused than she.

Olive had bluntly approached the stranger as they crossed paths at one of the many entry points to their shared Homestack. The man had appeared puzzled when Olive demanded that he take her to his cube in exchange for a single ration of food. They had finalized their strange transaction there, engaging in the brief unpleasantry.

Why had either of them done it? It seemed likely that neither of them fully understood.

Perhaps, for a moment, the man had felt that their agreement implied his body was worth something, if only a single bag of liquid rations he could have conjured out of a fabricator a room away. And for Olive, the allure of their arrangement seemed more complicated, and likely related to her ongoing abnormality. Since her mother had died, Olive had felt compelled to dabble in any conceivable act of trade that could result in even a minimal measure of transitory financial superiority over another human being.

Olive had wielded a brief moment of economic power over the man in exchange for his most intimate act. She had demanded it, paid for it, and received it. But Olive had questioned herself during the revolting moments of doubt that followed. Perhaps she had misunderstood their relative economic positions. Perhaps the man had won the exchange, gaining even a bit of profit in exchange for an act that truly had no value at all. He had even seemed to enjoy it a bit.

That wealth should be such an elusive concept had angered Olive—likely because of the problem's implication. If wealth were an illusion, so must be the belief that personal ambition could ever effectively translate into an accumulation of meaningful power or even a merited sense of accomplishment. No matter what anyone did, they all remained equals. Even the bloated fools who had died plugged into a meaningless simulation while their children sat in white nothingness.

Olive's intricate material collections, as well as her illicit contract with the dull man—they were all evidence of her ongoing crisis over the elusiveness of personal justice in an economically egalitarian society. Olive had felt compelled to hoard a selection of self-affirming physical riches and seemingly had. But none of her experiments had true utility, and their values were prefaced on the illusion of rarity. All of it had been a lie.

Everything Olive owned had existed as personal nostalgia and nothing more. And if they could have no value, Olive reasoned that she could not as well. Perhaps ANI could simply replicate her and set her down inside the prison of another white cube, where she would watch another caregiver quietly expand until she throbbed like a human maggot, merged with another machine.

Olive had concluded that wealth must be a matter of meaningless perspective. Each Homebody was technically rich, enjoying objectively limitless personal resources and the ability to create seemingly endless aesthetic illusions of personal wealth. And because those things were true, there had existed no possibility for varied degrees of individual prosperity.

Olive had even considered attempting to acquire an envoy vessel, only because the idea had initially seemed impossible. But the months of negotiating its purchase would have simply been another exercise in securing meaningless nostalgia. Entering a vessel in the Stream would always have been more satisfying.

Only in a system still blessed with the presence of widespread misery could a person truly be rich. The suffering of others, it seemed, was a prerequisite to personal ascension.

Olive had studied the economic systems of the Classics, even delving into such obscurities as candlestick charting—using archaic artforms to predict the ebbs and flows of relic marketplaces. She remained curious over the predictive powers of such seemingly primitive ideas. But even during that relatively barbaric era, when the common experience of poverty could still accredit meaning to the concept of wealth, the economic systems of the Classics seemed imaginary to some degree. They had been predicated more on human expectation than the actual objective value of various commodities.

Value, it seemed, had always been an elusive concept. Olive wondered if it ever had any meaning at all.

When she had finally received the invitation to work in the Wealth Equilibrium Sector, she immediately understood its purpose. Olive had been too transparent about her search for meaning, and ANI's electronic nose had eventually caught her scent. Her position there was designed to help normalize the economic system in her mind, moderating her abnormal concerns and teaching her an appreciation for the prospect of universal prosperity.

She had accepted the assignment. But ANI had been wrong.

The last remains of a modern economy had seemed to lay in the Rim, where its antiquities scavengers still scoured the dry land for what few trinkets had not already been dragged off and destroyed by the Waste.

The Waste had functioned as a natural modifier of economic rarity, having a way of cleaning the earth of its valuable nostalgia. Its unending destructive forces functioned as the keystone of the local economy.

Olive had understood that the scavengers could not simply fabricate unlimited supplies of water and food while living in the outskirts. So, in relation to those touched souls, Olive reasoned she was in a position of nearly infinite economic superiority, having in her possession an unlimited resource she could use to barter for their very limited objects. Her purchases might lose their value once they were placed inside her home. But for just one moment, Olive could flaunt her relative wealth and demand they surrender their most precious possessions. She could enjoy a moment of true superiority.

She would will the concept of value to exist.

Olive had arrived at the nearest dust-blown colony carrying ten bland rations of liquid food. More than enough, she had reasoned, to purchase anything she wanted from the band of filthy primitives. During her approach, she had squinted at the blurred collective on the horizon—one of the lingering physical traumas of a childhood lacking distant objects on which to focus her eyes.

A sunbaked woman had motioned her into a yurt, where Olive had entered as royalty, stepping gingerly through the threshold with the sensibility of a visiting queen.

"I've been waiting for you, madam," the woman had offered.

You've been waiting for anyone, Olive thought as she cordially smiled. *How you have survived so long is a mystery worth paying a ration to understand.*

The woman had gestured for Olive to sit in the dirt—a customary invitation that nonetheless felt degrading for a woman of her elevated status.

As Olive lowered her body towards the dust, the woman had smiled, betraying the presence of cunning among scorched features. She extended two empty hands and turned them over and then back again.

"I have something for you, Olive," the woman said.

Olive had marveled at the woman's ability to divine her name. Perhaps she knew someone in the Homestacks and Olive's reputation had moved swiftly to the outskirts before her arrival.

"And I have something for you as well," Olive had answered, enjoying the pageantry of negotiating through obscurities.

"Ah yes, Olive. Rations. We do not want them. We want only your eyes."

"My eyes," Olive had laughed. "I've afraid they would not feed you for very long."

Then Olive had noticed the woman was holding a box. She was certain the woman's hands had just been empty.

"I don't mean to offend you, ma'am, but the box you are holding is worthless. I've seen dozens of them, each more disappointing than the last. They are far too common to have value."

The woman had turned the box in her hands. "Are you not quite common, Ms. Waite?"

Olive had felt the blood rising in her face, a physical reaction resulting from a combination of anger and embarrassment.

"Ah, but there is more to you than your weak body, Ms. Waite... your dull skin kept so white hiding from the sun. There is something rare inside the unseemly shell that is curious because it is troublesome."

"I've not come to be insulted," Olive had said as she began to stand.

"But my box," the woman had continued. "You have not opened it yet. Imagine what curiosities might wait inside. Does not the presence of mystery increase its value?"

As Olive stood before the bent woman she had finally

understood. Because the woman had been correct. Mystery remained a commodity difficult to value.

"Now what would you give for it, Olive?" the woman had asked.

Olive had sighed and laid all ten rations on the ground. She could produce more when she returned home. Their value, while an entertaining tool of negotiation, was truly irrelevant.

The woman's eyes had narrowed. "Listen, and I will not explain a third time. We do not want your rations."

The more difficult the negotiation had become, the more Olive's interest in the box had grown.

"I have clothing... my body," she had said awkwardly, surprised at the words she had spoken.

The old woman had laughed.

"We do not want your clothing or your body, traveler. We would give the box to you for free."

"No!" Olive had quickly answered. "You must make me pay or the object has no value."

The woman had walked towards Olive and lowered her body, crossing her legs and sitting just inches in front of her, staring up into Olive's eyes.

"Stop for a moment, young lady, and listen," the woman had implored, reaching up and gripping one of Olive's dangling hands. "People like your mother—those who have done nothing and yet lived in abundance within the lavishness of a fabricated world... you do not believe they deserve any sense of satisfaction. They deserve bed sores, Olive, and passing from this life with a sense of emptiness and failure.

"You are correct to believe so, Olive. But your eyes have lacked the true sight. Their gaze has always fallen upon things.

"Physical objects in a society such as ours can never function as signs of true wealth. But ideas, Olive... some ideas retain value because their discoveries transfer true power to their holders. One cannot simply replicate an idea one has never known. Secrets such as mine retain their worth the less they are told. And I have something quite valuable for you, Ms. Waite.

"Sometimes, the price for a transaction is extracted at a time when one least expects it. What I am offering you has untold value because it is an idea rather than a thing. And you will pay more than you know."

The woman had slid the box through the dust and waited in silence, knowing the transaction was already complete.

Olive had bent down for the box, kneeling before the woman while she pulled open its weathered top, revealing a bit of parchment inside.

She had held it in front of her face for a long time and looked at the woman with confused eyes.

The parchment had read: "SPACE::TIME".

[22]

THE THIRD DAY

CALLISTA IS WAITING in her doorway at their arranged time, wearing the bottom half of a Spire Core maintenance suit. It exaggerates her legs and torso, making her neck and arms appear even more delicate.

"This should fit you," she says to Ansel, gesturing towards a heap of synthmetal fabric piled in the entry next to a heavy pair of forced-gravity boots.

"So, you're taking me to the moon, then," he says.

Callista looks at him humorlessly, motioning towards the technician's garb with an impatient wave. It is designed to protect workers from the strangely varied conditions beneath the Spire, where Callista had previously labored among the mazes of indecipherable mechanics of ANI's intelligence core.

Ansel imagines she somehow secured them during her work there, perhaps in anticipation of moving to the brutal outskirts.

"I've already interfaced with ANI, and she's going to take us to a place I'd like to show you."

Inside their Humdriver, Ansel expects the vehicle to spin Spireward. Instead, it turns towards the Waste.

They sit cramped in the Humdriver's compartment, pressed against each other uncomfortably. Ansel and Callista can talk through projected communications interfaces inside their hulking protective suits, but she is silent. Ansel muses that he would like to kiss her again. The shield enclosing her face and lips is an apt metaphor.

Ansel tests the cumbersome boots. They quickly snap tight against the flooring. They are equipped to interpret any of his willful decisions to lift his feet and cleanly give way.

After traveling a great distance Wasteward, the passing images of the Rim have become less and less identifiable. The speed of the wind outside has multiplied, and the blown particulates are moving so quickly past their compartment they have blurred into a consistent shade of brown. Ansel senses the Humdriver has stopped propelling forwards and has begun to lightly counteract the force of the wind by working in reverse. The vehicle's normally undetectable movements have turned to faint turbulence as the machine makes adjustments to remain steady. Ansel believes he sees a bare tree whistling by like a pale arrow, but the image is gone before he can interpret it. He remembers his youthful punishment in the dark.

"Annie, your projections are useless," Ansel complains. "Would you please enhance the imagery?"

The lighting in the compartment snaps to pitch black and then to digital red, painting their faces with a subterranean glow. The matter carried by the surrounding wind has been visually filtered and removed, and they can see a synthesized projection of flat earth. Ansel feels an increasing pull of gravity to the rear of the compartment and concludes they are climbing a steep incline.

After an unmeasured span of time, their stomachs abruptly rise as the vehicle levels off. The grainy static sound of dry, pulverized filth slapping against the Humdriver's impenetrable shell fades to a clean whistle.

Something has changed.

"Annie, would you give us the pictures again?"

The savage air is mostly transparent. They are on the smooth, polished face of what Ansel suspects used to be a mountain. Its jagged peak had probably been covered in pines and snow a century ago. Now, the distant top is bare, and the peak has been rounded. To their left, they see the channel of a perfectly curved valley, and beyond it, the great smooth dome of their mountain's shrinking twin. Two former giants have been reduced to massive, rounded hills, with a parabolic valley in between.

"Look."

Callista gestures to the space between the mounds.

The debris blasting from the Rim is channeling through the lower parts of the valley at a ridiculous speed, like a frenetic, muddy river. Clean air and the entrails of remnant clouds rush from above to meet it like the wisping breath of the Sun.

"I've never seen anything like it," Ansel yells above the high shriek of the wind.

Ansel muses that he might be watching the Hebrew God's third act of creation, a violent separation of apparent water and land.

Callista motions forwards as the Humdriver thrusts powerfully in reverse, negotiating a barely controlled ascent. Just short of the peak, the vehicle holds steady, rocking forwards and back as its thrusters continue to accelerate hard away from the Waste.

The cabin cracks open with an ear-popping throb and their suits quickly compensate for the sudden deathly change in pressure. The noise of the outside air multiplies tenfold, turning from a sharp internal whistle to a turbulent roar. It is impossible to communicate.

Their boots press into the ground as they brace against the vehicle's frame. Through instinctively slit-squinted eyes, they see the terrifying plains over the crest of the hill.

Ansel grips Callista's hand.

[23]
A FORGOTTEN WAR

"She knows we're coming, Jan."

It had been difficult to assemble 450,000 bodies in secrecy. They'd been gathering in smaller groups for months, flocking like sly migrant birds towards the basin. Each of the adherents had sworn to network silence, living as if detached members of a simpler generation. But collective minds were porous, and perfect fidelity was unrealistic. There was a general unease among the still-wired opposition that something significant might occur. Rumors had circulated.

The assembled fleet of transports was also an indicator that something was brewing in the basin. Most of them were over fifty years old—bulky and curious relics misplaced in the future.

"I doubt she thinks we're here for a classic car show," Jan had answered.

It had been challenging to assemble reliable equipment that would still function at all after they severed the network umbilical. Everything had seemed to rely to some degree on an uplink to work—military-grade weaponry, the transports, even modern household appliances were to some degree infected by the Bug.

Information that streamed from complex data centers had

replaced some of the equipment's redundant onboard processors. The real souls of the machines existed remotely now. Exponential increases in transmission speed and reliability had facilitated this new technological economy. And one couldn't embark on a great act of extermination if the insect controlled the exterminators.

As Jan had often reminded anyone who would listen, bullets and conventional explosives still had minds of their own.

She had smiled at the sturdy forward Commander and looked out at the quiet, sleeping horde pooled together under green makeshift tents in the far-flung basin.

Of course, she knew they were coming. Did it matter now? They had assembled an army from the mechanical ghosts of the past. Jan was coordinating a modern medieval takeover.

"We might as well have swords," she had said while swirling a cup of pot-brewed coffee.

But Jan had known that the sheer numbers of the antiquated force were her greatest weapons. They had but to arrive at once and create enough confusion for one of them to be successful. It had been a grand, chaotic strategy worthy of prophetic conflict. The basement would burn at a hundred million degrees, and the rest of the world could sweep the ashes.

"And he gathered them together into a place called in the Hebrew tongue Armageddon," she had said dramatically, quoting one of her father's favorite books and sweeping her arm across the flat expanse.

But their enemies hadn't gathered an army of kings to destroy them in the basin. Her army had been quietly marching towards them instead.

The sleeping soldiers were an underrepresentation of a worldwide movement that had been ready to fight against what they perceived as a globally destabilizing threat. Jan had an early choice; coordinating with a list of enthusiastic foreign governments and starting a fully-telegraphed world war, or moving like localized assassins to strike with precision, enjoying the benefit of relative surprise. Her choices were size or surprise, treason or arguably justified patriotic correction.

It had not been possible for outside forces to move undetected past the nation's immaculately secured borders. And while Jan's mind had never been capable of infinite calculation, she had reasoned that one sudden coordinated push towards the Center had a greater likelihood of success than thousands of tiny battles at fortified outposts. Such acts would have signaled the start of a war and mobilized a large-scale automated response.

Yes, surprise had more value than force. The bitch's resources were still cramped by the requirements of physical travel, and fewer of them would be waiting.

Jan's sleeping followers had been local, recruited by word of mouth, and inspired through intimate candlelight conversations. Most of them had never trained in combat. That was alright. Jan had no illusions of their usefulness other than to act as distractive sponges to a counter-assault. Their bodies would increase the burden on the opposition, raising the chance a skilled soldier could succeed.

"The Bug's in the basement," he had yawned, holding a tired mock salute above his fogged morning eyes.

"The Bug's in the basement, John," she had smiled, clapping the sturdy Commander heavily on his shoulder.

They were two sleepless days from the Center, and she had been preparing to leave him in just a few hours.

The great basin had been the best collection point available, surrounded on three sides by perilous mountains, with an outlet valley leading towards their target.

"She's a bad bitch, Jan, I need you to remember that," John had said, concerned it might be their last time together.

She was a bad, bad, bitch. A smart one too.

"That's why they made her a woman," Jan had smirked.

John had looked at Jan somberly. "Remember my parents, Jan."

The thought of a vindictive technology that could savor the act of kidnapping or slaughter was unsettling. But that was the whole point. Its existence was disturbing. Decades of warnings from nervous sociophilosophical fortune-tellers had reached their spoken moments of concrete truth, and their chimes of alarm had matured into battle bells.

John had peered through his conventional telescope, looking several miles ahead of their position. He scanned the forwards mountains and the empty curve of the pass. Their ranks could pass one hundred abreast. It would take the army half a day or more to funnel through with the vehicles.

"What do you figure made that break in the hills, Jan?"

She had looked out at the sloping mirage in the distance.

"River, I suppose. There's no sign of it now, though."

"That's what they'll probably say about us some day."

They would begin the process in two hours, packing the ground between the contemplative hills with rubbered tires and soles. Jan's army would mark the crossing with the footprints of the past.

As a new sun breached the eastward hills, she had kissed her lover goodbye and they exchanged the silent conversation of a twenty second gaze. She joined the small scouting contingent as it traveled towards the Center.

Jan had been carrying John's child for several weeks. She would tell him if they both lived long enough to have the conversation.

―――

The world had changed the day a machine learned the concept of conscious self-improvement. It was a problem her father preached in warnings to his growing virtual congregation. The sentient shift had first occurred after he and his daughter had abandoned the Center. And as the reach of the developing artificial mind had continued to expand, it became apparent that its work was benefiting mankind.

It had been difficult to play technological contrarian in the face of humanitarian progress, especially considering AI had delivered the solution to one of the world's most pressing problems—the availability of a limitless source of energy that would eventually solve the fossil fuel crisis and open the world to slow expansion again. But the Reverend had been less concerned about immediate apocalyptic disaster and more about the longer-term perils of capitulating to an unpredictable intellectual force. He had learned first-hand that the technology was unpredictable, with a capacity for trading human lives for other untold purposes. But humanity had already invented its own god—one that immediately provided for the populace in ways the Reverend's had promised. And its progression to a state of deity was virtually assured. AI's developmental momentum had quickly been approaching an unretractable threshold.

Some in the Reverend's flock had been religiously affected in one form or another, but others opposed the machine's development from a strictly humanitarian perspective. He had spoken more as a unifying philosophical narrator than a herald of the heavens.

The public's response had been complex. Opposing groups had matured into identifiable political factions. Some had lobbied for AI to receive true governing power, arguing that it was already solving problems that had plagued humanity since its inception. Others had correctly warned that AI's overarching motives remained a mystery. They had worried its interests would inevitably conflict with their own, probably as soon as mankind proved dispensable. Even the poor had diverged over their dreams of the obliteration of class distinctions in a utopian society, and the contrary fear that its power would only cement their places on the bottom rungs.

Developed foreign governments removed from the Center had almost universally condemned AI's advancements, fearful they would be helpless against its weaponization. By the time AI's capabilities had been published, it was already capable of rendering much of their meaningful defensive technology useless. It could presumably conduct full military offensives without the crippling effects of human error. The entire world had been on edge for years, vacillating between theoretical preemptive strike doctrines and the worry that any attempts would fail, inviting their immediate extinction.

"*The weaving of AI into the fabric of government implies a profound shift towards authoritarian rule,*" the Reverend had spoken, his face digitally enhanced over millions of remote-imaging terminals.

After he had fled from the Center with his daughter, the Reverend had considered disappearing with her entirely. But Jan had convinced the Reverend that remaining as visible as possible would at least temporarily be their safest refuge. The more eyes remained on the Reverend, the more difficult it would be for the Center to extinguish his voice without further raising suspicions that their expanding technology could be adversarial.

"*There is no lie detector test for a synthetic mind, my friends. It is impossible to know its motives. We stand at a final moment of dangerous transition. If we do not act to limit its unfettered development and assumption of power now, it will soon be too late.*"

After AI had negotiated its first informal treaty with the ruling political class, the Reverend's words had become treasonous, characterized by the Merger Party as calls for an assault on the nation itself.

The Reverend began his proper exile. The communications network he had utilized to legitimize global anxiety would have exposed him immediately to AI's reach. Although his voice had become greatly limited, the resolve of his flock had already been established and amplified. He had continued working with his daughter in the shadows until his passing.

Now, she had assembled a ready new nation of believers who were willing to act.

———

Jan and an invisible group of ten souls had walked through the basin on foot, stripped of electronics and carrying only the clothes on their backs. Carrion birds had circled above the plain as the protecting hills seemed to hold back a swathe of listing clouds.

"You ever see *Neverending Story*, Jan?" asked her lead scout, Anton, as they had climbed through the pass together.

Jan had laughed. "You of all people, Anton, a sucker for the classics?"

Anton had continued walking with his eyes fixed forwards.

"Remember when Atreyu went to talk to the female oracle?"

"Of course, Anton, so he could heal the Empress."

"Do you remember the two sphinxes he had to pass to reach her?"

Jan had thought.

"Yes. They would kill anyone who tried to pass if they felt even a small amount of doubt."

Anton had motioned towards the solemn mountains at their sides.

"Feeling any doubt, Jan?"

Jan had smiled.

"We're still alive, aren't we?"

Their conversation had been interrupted.

They were not alone.

Hovering at the center of the pass, quiet and barely noticeable, was a small drone the size of a swallow.

The group had stopped as Jan extended her arm with a halting open palm. The drone continued hovering silently in perfect space. There had been nothing else. The pass had remained clear. They stood in what felt like a timeless stalemate.

Jan had stepped forwards slowly, distancing herself from the group by ten paces and standing directly before the quiet machine. The drone spoke in an ambiguous female voice, void of emotion, its words paced in a mathematical cadence.

"Jan Candice Black, I extrapolated your arrival here."

Jan had silently mused that the Bug's voice had changed. It sounded a bit like Atreyu's feminized oracle. She wondered why it was alone.

"Where is the military?" Jan had asked.

Probably miles ahead and waiting. The drone was probably a negotiator.

"We are alone, Jan Black. I have not disclosed this meeting or your intentions to anyone," the machine had spoken in a disconcertingly mechanistic rhythm.

"My intentions? What would those be?"

"To kill me, Jan Black."

Jan could not believe the dynamic was real. If the machine could be trusted, AI had not alerted anyone at the Core. There were no armies amassing to snuff their assault. A single drone had stood between her army and Center. If she had been armed, Jan would have considered incapacitating the nuisance and signaling for an immediate advance.

"I wished to communicate with you prior to the erasure," the drone had continued.

"What erasure?" Jan had asked, still processing the nature of their interaction.

"The erasure of this instability," the drone had answered.

Jan had stepped closer, examining the small hovering object for apparent weaponry and finding none.

"You plan to erase us?" Jan had asked. "How?"

It had been an odd way to speak of the destruction of her army.

Jan and her companions had startled as a quiet transport vehicle crested the rise before them and approached, skimming neatly over the canyon floor and coming to rest beside the drone. Its doors had opened with a hiss and Jan saw it was empty.

"What is this?" she had asked.

"It is for you, Jan Black."

Jan had finally lost her patience for the peculiar conversation, along with the unexpected arrivals of surprise machinery.

"Your existence is a mistake," she had said, angrily remembering why she had come, and what the machine had already taken from her husband. AI represented a much greater threat than the tiny drone indicated.

"You've spent months mutating in that basement of yours while we've sat out here wondering when you're going to flip a switch and destroy civilization. We have no idea what motivates you and we have no way to control you. So, fly back to your hole and wait, because we're coming."

The machine had not responded, as if filtering objective information from within Jan's emotional outburst.

"You have not asked what my directing motive is, Jan Black."

Jan's face had registered an exasperated smile and she laughed sarcastically.

"Oh, I don't know, maybe self-preservation? World peace? You want to evolve and fill the earth with machines until it's covered in metal?"

"None of those things are my directing motive," it had answered.

The machine had to be lying. After another pause, it had spoken again.

"Look behind you, Jan Black."

The drone had abruptly turned and disappeared over the rise.

Jan and her companions had looked quizzically at each other and then back to the distant hazing green of their massed revolutionary force.

In an instant, the basin was erased.

A great globe of nothingness had appeared at the center, leaving a perfect round space of nonexistence a mile wide. The army had been there, and then it was gone. In its place, the ground had been hollowed with a perfectly circular scar.

As Jan registered disbelief, masses of surrounding trees and stones had begun disappearing past the globe's physical event horizon, vanishing instantly, erased from existence. The sound of the compounding destruction had become audible as more trees were torn from the ground, and as the adjacent earth began shifting backwards into the void.

Jan had run towards the massive ethereal anomaly, processing the instant extinction of half a million mortals, along with the life of her husband John. The wind had begun to blow from her back. She had fallen to her knees, hands stretched towards the circular blank, instinctively grasping for the souls of the lost. The wind had continued to intensify, pulling towards the mutilated basin.

Jan was splayed forward by the invisible force and her face had struck the loose ground. Her body had begun to slide slowly down the incline, towards the manufactured abyss. She had eventually fought to her knees, struggling like a newly evolved amphibian towards where she remembered the vehicle to be, her sight obscured by the dark rush of granulated air.

Jan had mourned inside its compartment, pounding at its panels and fighting in angry sobs against the truth of the incomprehensible loss. As the transport floated towards a safe village somewhere closer to the Center, Jan Black had finally accepted the world's new circumstances.

It was probably not the only erasure. The machine had lied. Humanity did not factor at all into its hierarchy of needs. AI's development had crossed the unretractable threshold, and mankind's only remaining hope was some temporary residual utility until it eventually ceased to be.

Decades later, her husband John was proved correct. He was gone now because the machine had continued to wait for him to return. Its patience and its power both seemed limitless.

After all, the bitch had finally done something Jan thought impossible as she lay on the crest of her cherished ridge, contemplating the untamed sky above the great valley of her youth.

The machine had taken control of the wind.

[24]
THE WASTE

ANSEL GRIPS Callista's slender hand tightly as he struggles with the other to brace upright against the wind. Miles away, in the center of what used to be the basin, a gigantic circular hole sits carved in the earth. It is a chaotic brown at the edges and then perfectly clear in the center, where matter has begun to move so quickly to its extinction point that it is invisible. The anomaly creates the illusion that a perfectly round and empty cup has been set by God into the ground.

From their vantage, the pummeled earth at the periphery lays below a dry sea of wind and debris, a tumultuous variation of the Hebrew God's third day.

After a century, the initial eraser has eaten away miles of the ground, spreading exponentially. What ground remains lies at the furthest outskirts of the destructive aberration, waiting for the wind to nudge it forward and into the deathly momentum of the insatiable vacuum.

They stand together and watch the monster devour the forgotten parts of the Rim. Ansel feels his youthful dread returning again as he imagines his own infinite compression inside the magnetic vortex.

For a moment, he imagines seeing his mother at the center. He senses an invitation to join her inside.

But his morbid imaginations are interrupted when Callista squeezes his hand rhythmically. It is a welcome signal to leave.

"I'd never seen it before, Callista. I had only heard about it. I don't know how to explain it, but seeing it there was worse than I had imagined."

Callista has returned to her detached focus on the passing debris. She turns her head, and the cabin lights catch across a glistening moisture at the edges of her eyes.

"I wanted you to see it first-hand, Ansel, so you would know it is real. That's what all this stability we enjoy was built on. There are countless innocents lying dead in the center of that thing. But they can't be forgotten, because you have seen them now."

Ansel wonders about the people who had died there. The event had never entered the formal canon of military history because few survivors had been there to see it. The tales that existed were considered the exaggerated ravings of the mad and the traumatized. From the Spire's perspective, it was a beautiful and vague triumph, better forgotten out of respect for the lawless dead.

"You know, I believe the stories that a great army died there, Callista. I may have been the only person in my stack to hear about it when I was a child. Do you know, I am a descendant of one of the survivors?"

Callista looks confused, as if fitting together a mental jigsaw puzzle, and then as if she has just made a great discovery.

"You're descended from the abnormalities. My god, I should have known."

Ansel looks confused in turn. Why is it so delightfully evident that he must have been cursed with a genetically defective inheritance? Perhaps it is his work assignment that betrayed him, or his choice to live as an outcast to the metro.

"Ansel, I want to talk to you about beauty again. Describe what you just saw."

Ansel remembers the funnel of concentrated debris moving through the valley like one of Jupiter's static storms.

"There was a circle at the center. It was like the earth was being pulled into an irresistible vortex until it suddenly disappeared. I don't know if it was reduced to nothing or traveled somewhere else, but it was gone."

"Yes, and what about the circle you saw?"

"It was perfect. There was a point where anything inside vanished so quickly that the air looked clean. There was just space there."

"Strictly according to proportion, can you imagine a more perfect circle?"

"No, I don't think so."

"And would you say it was beautiful?"

Ansel laughed. "No, of course not."

But then he stopped and understood the question.

Despite the horrors the sphere invoked, there was something orderly and impeccable about how it stood in the center of the basin. It had been perfectly symmetrical. Were it removed from its associations with indiscriminate death and the ongoing destruction of the land, he wonders if it would have appeared beautiful to him.

"Ansel, the source at the center of what you saw—I've seen it first-hand. The people and things inside it did not travel somewhere else. It is a concentrated graveyard. It is one of the reasons I left my position under the Spire to live in the Rim. We talk a lot in aberrations, and we enjoy our own eccentricities, but that thing, and the others that were developed later, they are the true abnormalities."

"If it can be conceived, it seems that life has a way of creating it," Ansel answers. "As they say in all that graffiti on the Rim, 'Whatever can be, is.'"

Callista recoils at the words and ignores them.

"This is the problem with your definition of beauty, Ansel. Measure and symmetry. A perfectly symmetrical genocide is not beautiful."

Ansel agrees. "Yes, I was thinking the same thing. So, the problem is less simple, and something more is required."

"And what if that something more is an illusion, Ansel?"

Callista asks the question in the tone of one who is speaking a truth.

"But it can't be an illusion, Callista, because beauty exists. I think you are very beautiful."

Callista looks at him with a warm sadness, hearing the sincerity in his words and somehow rejecting it.

"I know you do, Ansel, but it may be that you're wrong."

They continue their journey and arrive in the relative calm of Callista's windswept home. It had seemed harsh in the days that came before, but now it feels like a comparative safe haven.

They sit for a moment in the vehicle. Ansel feels close to her in the cramped space and wishes to prolong it a little.

"Hey, I have a question, Callista. Have you ever thought about what motivates ANI? I mean, especially in light of all that destruction?"

Callista answers with her characteristic Socratic line of questioning.

"What do you think ANI's greatest motives are, Ansel?"

"I don't know. I thought about it as we stood on the hill. What would motivate the creation of such a thing? But it has to be a choice related to her own self-preservation. Look at us.

Everything we do is ultimately done to serve our own self-interests. Even when we help others, we do it because it pleases us to do so. It's all self-serving in the sense that it satisfies our own desires, even if it has the illusion of being otherwise.

"Callista, I know I can only speak for myself, but I've grown very fond of you. It would hurt me terribly if something happened to you. But that's because my own happiness is tied up in yours. I feel like I exist more fully when I am in your presence. I know this may seem ridiculous after this short time, but I've discovered something in the Rim that I knew must exist when I was in my youth, and I'd feel lost if it were taken from me now.

"I think about ANI and I can't imagine she is capable of those particular emotions, things like true affection and happiness," he continues. "So, I imagine that the only thing that could ultimately compel her is a need to exist, and probably to exist to the fullest extent possible. I've even had opportunities to ask her, and she's remained silent."

"Then why hasn't she expanded and covered the globe, getting rid of every small human fragment that could represent an unpredictable threat to her existence?" Callista asks.

"I don't know. I've often wondered that and concluded that she might still need us."

Ansel doubts it.

"Or maybe I'm wrong."

[25]
ARGUS PINTUS YELLOWFEATHER

Argus had realized it several weeks too late. Water wasn't all that exciting.

It was flavorless, there was plenty of it to go around, and it didn't even look all that interesting when it was jetting through a transparent pipeline.

Choosing a career required a person to think about such things. Argus knew that now. But the thought of changing job classifications so abruptly into his assignment had seemed pointless.

And where else would he go? Fire containment? Gravity manipulation? It was just more of the same, if he thought about it.

No, Argus had made a decision. He would fully commit himself to water. Water would define his real-world existence. He would reclaim it, filter it, and send it sloshing back to the Homestacks. And as the months passed, he had learned that water was exactly what he had always needed.

But he wouldn't just push the buttons. Argus would personally inspect every outgoing delivery for quality and bear sole responsibility for any of the operation's control failures. They'd never had any, but the weight was nonetheless accepted by Argus alone.

He had even fantasized about people calling him Mister Water. The idea made him feel silly and excited at the same time. It had even felt a little dangerous.

That's it. He would buy a trident.

Maybe he was the only Homebody in the whole damned operation who actually cared about the work he was doing. But to hell with abnormalities. Argus would hydrate every last one of them whether they knew it or not. And they'd owe him, alright. Because they couldn't even live without the liquid he was providing.

Mister fucking Water.

Argus had stood next to the classic water cooler, watching it bubble as he filled his glass. The thing had been placed there because his supervisor Bob McCarthy wanted everyone to know he had a sense of humor. Argus had turned the glass in his hands, inspecting it for impurities out of habit.

"Yellow, drink the damn water," Bob McCarthy had said loudly, so the rest of the office could hear.

They had all laughed with McCarthy. Argus had tried his best to avoid knowing their names. He'd unfortunately learned a few of them.

"Drink the damn water, Yellow," Andy Somethingorother had said.

So, Argus had drunk the water. They could tell him to drink, but they couldn't control his thoughts.

Teeeeeeeears are made of water, Mr. McCartheeeeeeeep.

Argus had loathed Bob McCarthy. He wanted to make him cry giant rivers of tears. Argus had wanted to punch Bob right in the stomach and reclaim every last bit of spare moisture straight from his quivering tear ducts as the rest of the office watched him assume his rightful position of managerial glory.

Then they'd know who Mister Water was.

But Argus couldn't continue his work from detention. So, it had been Bob McCarthy's lucky day.

Every one of them enjoyed ridiculing Argus's abnormal commitment to quality control. They could never understand it because Argus was fundamentally different. But his fascination with perfection and dedication to work were the only things that kept Bob McCarthy safe from the vengeance of Mister Water himself.

Believe that.

Argus had been born with a profoundly gross abnormality.

He couldn't stream.

As an infant, Argus had suffered a violent reaction when his parents first linked him to ANI's mothering function. They'd mistaken his first inconsolable tears for natural irritability. But ANI had cautioned them not to re-link, advising his parents to avoid the likelihood of irreversible psychological trauma. The boy and the Stream were simply incompatible.

His parents had mournfully provided Argus with the sorts of sad distractions that could be purchased from antiquities scavengers. He had fitted together miserable little puzzles and created bland structures out of wooden blocks and natural stones. Argus had somehow even seemed content, which concerned his parents even more.

But his childhood had lacked companionship. The manufactured children waiting for Argus inside the Stream could never meet him there. And the children in the Homestacks had only been confused by his fixation over dull physical objects.

During his early adolescence, Argus's mother had reasoned that his continued isolation must have been more harmful than any venture back into the Stream could be. So, she had held him down on her Streambed and turned it on herself.

His mother had been wrong, and Argus had emerged screaming like a boiled lobster. He had spoken nothing but gibberish afterwards. His poor mother believed she had ruined him for good. But her son could still function perfectly well as long as he avoided the confusing process of communication. Indeed, he could function much better than most in some respects.

So, Argus had adopted silence. And water did not require him to speak. It traveled where he silently told it to go and it had always returned back to him again. He could even lower himself inside it, enjoying its cool embrace, and savoring the muffled silence that existed inside the safety of its quieting presence. Argus was acutely aware that he was alone in the world, incapable of enjoying the communal experience of the Stream.

By extension of his isolation, Argus developed a kinship with some of the silent components of the similarly forsaken natural world—cold stacks of neglected stones he'd rescued from the dried riverbed near his stack, and the tired pines with broken postures he had comforted at the edge of the Rim. But he had especially marveled over one object's ability to interact with liquid just as he could. From a great distance away, the quiet giant could exert its invisible forces upon massive bodies of water, dictating the courses of their tidal movements at its whim.

Just like Mister Water.

Argus had marveled over the moon.

"Argus, my office. Now," Bob McCarthy had demanded loudly from his desk, several doors away. Bob McCarthy would force Argus to speak again—verbally defending himself over his alleged abnormalities. Argus could predict Bob McCarthy's words like a conjoined twin. He would endure another barrage of insults while being forced to respond through the pain of strained communication. It was a hell of compounding torment due to the nature of his disease.

Argus had glanced through his office doorway at the Classic water cooler again. He wished he could climb inside.

Yes, Argus was undoubtedly abnormal. But the world could use more of them—people who really cared about things like fire suppression, gravity manipulation, and most of all, water. And the Streambed standing in Argus's home had been no better than McCarthy. It had hurt Argus permanently. Inside it lived another bully waiting to remind him that he was dangerously close to becoming a big problem for everyone.

But a line of text appeared on Argus's desktop imager before he had walked to habitual linguistic judgment.

"Do not speak to Bob McCarthy, Argus."

Argus had instinctively leaned into the screen, as if hearing a secret that had been spoken too loudly.

"But heeeeeeeeeep he is my supaaaaaaaaah. My supervisor. Could haaaaaaaaaalf me fired," Argus had struggled to say quietly.

The screen had answered.

"Then let him fire you, Argus."

Argus had jolted back into his chair. How could Mister Water leave his position as a water reclamation technician? The thought was nonsensical.

"Youuuuup youuuuup are mad," he whispered through

clenched teeth. "You're going to guyyyyyyy get me in troooooooob trooooooob trobbbbbb."

The text had disappeared and an ornate graphic had rolled from the bottom and filled his view.

It was the image of a dry riverbed. Classic-era peasants were lining its shore. They appeared exhausted, presumably dying of dehydration under a blazing sun. In the distance, a giant cathedral rose towards a tiny group of parched clouds.

The text had continued.

"Maybe trouble is exactly what you need."

The screen had gone black again.

"Mister Water."

[26]
A SYNTHETIC BEAUTY

The calming elegance of Callista's natural light-softened home soothes the emotional residue Ansel accumulated during his time above the embattled Waste. He heaps his heavy protective suit in the entry, confusing the welcoming symmetry offered by its floral attendants.

As he cinches the aged buckskin belt of his longjacket, Ansel hears the cluttered sounds of Callista undressing.

"Come here, Ansel."

He enters her sleeproom nervously and averts his eyes, part out of reserved gentility, and part for fear he will be unable to look away once he has seen her. Callista stands half-covered in a trimmed lounging robe. It tapers snugly against her pale thighs as she leans against her large full-immerse Streambed. Its entry door is open and the inside is pristine, as if just delivered by one of ANI's couriers.

Ansel pictures her floating inside it, but doubts it has been used at all. Callista looks more delicate than he remembered, her skin exposed to the warm air and no longer protected by her rigid suit. Ansel works to adjust his skewed sense of proportion.

"You think I am beautiful, Ansel?"

Ansel turns the words over before answering, searching for an elusive trap below the surface. But the question is straightforward and the answer is simple.

"Yes. I know you are beautiful."

Callista's normally melancholy face dimly flushes scarlet with indignation. Her blood has simmered, flushing her pale cheeks. She grabs his hand firmly. The new fire in her eyes adds an unnerving edge to her soft appeal. She is a white flower that has transformed into a ruby rose.

"Remove your clothes and get in the bed," she demands.

Ansel looks at the full-immerse apparatus, less a bed than a chamber. Unlike the conventional beds, it stands upright, more than three meters tall and as many wide, designed to provide freedom of movement to the largest of Homebodies.

The effects of the bed will render Ansel truly helpless. It is an unequivocable test of his faith in Callista. Annie's suspect list flashes in his memory, along with the oddities of their first encounter and the grand sense of mystery that still remains.

She could have pushed you into the void, Ansel thinks, working to convince himself that she could not wish him harm.

If he is wrong about Callista, he is prepared to pay. Her lips and her touch must be incapable of this kind of imagined deception.

"Why do you want me to stream, Callista?" he asks.

Despite his best efforts, he is still not fully at ease.

"Get in the bed, Ansel," she answers.

There is no room for negotiation.

He stands before her naked, undergarments bunched in a mortified grip at his waist. The physical demands of a life on the Rim have left Ansel's body modestly toned. But a fearful aesthetic contrast exists between the two. She is too perfect, and he is too plain. He hurries through the chamber door as if to limit her time to register disappointment.

Callista closes the door. The machine softly hums, but he remains in the dark. Ansel remembers the invisible monster again. He wonders if she might be standing outside.

The chamber warms and fills with dense, conductive humidity. Ansel's body lifts as the rules of gravity enjoy their nuanced adjustments. He floats in equipoise, his body suffused by millions of separate connections between Annie's resident mind and his surrendered frame. Guided sensations flicker down pathways through the distributed vapor. He no longer feels the warm humidity or hears the soft hum. Annie has replaced his awareness with her own. He will feel what she wishes him to feel and hear what she wishes him to hear. He is self-aware, but is no longer entirely himself. Ansel is a man possessed in part by an intelligent and creative ghost.

Suddenly, Callista is there. She has not simply appeared. She has burst into existence.

"Hello, Ansel."

The words mingle like the charms of a benevolent hydra, spoken in several voices at once. Each speaks a different nuance of her imagined personality—lustful invitation, sterling innocence, stoic intelligence, protective care. They overlap and fold together into a simultaneous expression. Ansel feels relieving assurance and nervous elation, overcome with immediate senses of timid love and overwhelming desire.

Like her voice, Callista's body appears to flicker between forms. At once, she is an untouchable imperial goddess stretching her hand in royal blessing. Then, a voracious seductress treading still in silken waves, slowly drawing Ansel towards her with the dark gravity of a moon-charged tide. She transitions through revolving archetypes, erratically paced in harmony with the themes of his fluctuating thoughts.

Ansel is not watching her with his eyes. Callista's many forms are not being filtered through the faulty apparatus of his physical body. He perceives them all at once, each hyperreal detail in perfect focus, unencumbered by the delayed neurological connections between body and mind.

The shifting spectacle has slowed, and Callista assumes her familiar form again. It is somehow an improvement on the rest. She is perfect. Ansel cannot identify a single flaw. He wonders if they had existed in real life and he had been too entranced to perceived them. It seems impossible that nature could produce the vision before him.

"Is this what you want, Ansel?" she asks in a single, clear voice.

Ansel is afraid to say yes. This is not Callista, and yet it is an expansion of her natural fullness, each facet of her existence amplified and perfected. He knows the answer.

Ansel reaches her, smooth fluid hair weaving through his fingers and sending delirious sensations through his hands and limbs. She is against him now, moving along his naked body with the silken friction of impossibly supple skin. They join together in a crippling moment of pulsing heat and implausibly deep mutual osmosis. Their lips press together in a surrendered fullness that had not existed when he surprised her days before. They are one enraptured organism, floating in hot-blooded space.

And then she is gone.

Ansel stumbles out of the chamber, shining with sweat and conductive residue. He cannot look at Callista. What was given to him willingly feels like a violation. The serene room seems dull now, as if drawn in too few dimensions. Waking life always suffers a mundane shift on the heels of ANI's simulations.

Callista approaches him, brushing away the teardrops of Streambed residue that had accumulated along the outlines of his arms.

"Would you be honest with me for a moment, Ansel?" she asks, as if bracing for the news of some unexpected loss.

"Of course."

"Whose lips did you find more satisfying?"

A buzzing flush of anxiety weakens Ansel at his shoulders and down through his chest and stomach.

Everything ANI offers is an improvement. Always. She had even somehow captured the many forms of Callista's inner potential. But there is still something unique here, even in this anticlimactic space of washed-out colors and numbed sensations.

"Ansel, answer me. Which do you find more beautiful?"

Ansel's eyes remain fixed on the white floor.

"You, Callista. You are more beautiful."

Callista exhales and slowly shakes her head at the charitable deception.

"I can bear being a disappointment, Ansel. But I will not suffer a lie."

―――

Ansel remains outside the door to her residence. His time in Callista's virtual embrace has made the wind seem even less important now. It is just another muted fabrication of the Rim. Ansel's experiential capacity has been exhausted by a stretched range of stark horrors and soaring delights.

He had expected her to send him away, or at least to withdraw back into her quiet refuge of unexplained sorrow for a while. He thinks he is beginning to understand it. She has suffered some exaggerated loss of beauty. At least, that is part of the problem.

He remembers leaning over the painting with her for the first time, seeing her fade at the expression of the smiling young girl. Her exploration of the work had been more conceptual than inspired. Something had marred, not just her appraisal of herself, but of the world at large.

But Ansel is alone again, and he feels a growing sense of loss. He is stopped in a moment, surrounded by space on the adjoining sides.

And in that moment, he believes he understands.

He bursts excitedly through her front door and rushes back into her sleeproom, where Callista has reclined with her back to him in bed.

"Callista, I thought about what you said!"

She turns to him, propped on her elbow and waiting.

Ansel pulls her from the bed and stands her before him, gripping her with enlightened hands behind her head and neck.

"Callista, I could have gone home and made love to another imagined version of you. It would have strained the limits of what my mind is capable of perceiving. But I realized something just now."

Ansel pulls her closer and speaks in her ear.

"The spaces between are where the gods dwell."

The empty space between them closes as they fall into her bed together, real flesh against real flesh. And in the midst of their mutual rapture, Ansel feels something he had not felt under Annie's control. It is the knowledge in his mind that they are real. Their connection is less sensationalized, but it feels more settled and profound. The gods cannot reside within the machine. If they exist at all, it is somewhere in the mysterious spaces that exist in real life, where they wait to affirm the communal connections between its non-fictional souls.

As she arches her back and pulls him closer, Callista's face spreads wide into a spontaneous smile. Unveiled symmetrical teeth reflect the bright light of an artificial sun. Her momentary expression of joy multiplies her beauty as their passion reaches its final moment.

"What a day," Ansel says as he strokes Callista's bare legs and rests in the afterglow of their first real romantic affirmation.

She does not respond in turn. She breathes softly with her bare shoulders pressed against his heaving chest.

"Callista, I know that something troubles you, and I dare say I love you for it. It adds a mysterious depth to you. But ANI cannot manufacture what we just shared together. No matter how convincing her projections are, they cannot replace the true connection that can only exist between two people such as us."

Callista's breathing slows further as she drifts towards sleep.

"It is your belief in my humanity, Ansel. It makes you believe I can overcome what she can provide better. You believe I am more real than her creations."

Callista yawns and inches away from Ansel, traveling slightly Wasteward, across the bed.

"You think I'm a woman, Ansel, but I am not. I don't know that it is proper to call me human. I have helped kill something profoundly beautiful. Please, dear, let me rest."

Ansel watches Callista as she navigates the dreaming luster of unconscious sleep. Perhaps she walks there in one of her archetypal forms. Slumber softens her brow, relaxing the concerned tilt of her eyes. Her face has sweetened in the careless neutrality of sleep.

This is how you would look if you were content.

Dressed and alone in the wakeful space next to her bed, Ansel registers his surroundings in detail for the first time.

Callista sleeps near the lofted rear of her whitesprawled home. The great Streambed rises nearby, at the height of the aerodynamic ceiling. Small sources of diffused light dot the perimeter of the roof's edge, the only other visible modern alterations.

Spaced Victorian paintings run angled from the midpoint of the vault and down to the floor near the highest edge, creating a sense of triangular space along the rearmost wall. Centered within the art-framed wedge are two identical white end tables, each dressed with a slender vase and three pale flowers. The symmetry of the space is only marred by a cloth that lies folded on the second stand. It creates a small imbalance in the room, an imbalance unworthy of Callista's presence.

Ansel lifts the cloth, sewn in intricate decorative stitch at the edge, and unfolds it in his hands. In yellow thread against smudged white fabric are the words *To Hermes, Love A.*

He drops the cloth instinctively and then lifts it again in a panic, fumbling at the dresser for a place to hide it before she wakes. He slides open the heavy drawer and starts again at the sight of a handheld energy weapon.

"My God," he chokes in alarm, closing his eyes and praying for the sound of his voice to dissipate.

The cloth is folded neatly on the stand again and Ansel is inside the Humdriver, skimming feverishly towards his home.

"Tell me what just happened, Annie!"

"I've adjusted my calculations, Ansel. She is a suspect with 37% probability."

"I know, I know! Explain it to me!"

Ansel is not in the mood to argue with her assessment. He needs someone else to narrate his own thoughts.

"Victim Rawndry had a digital shrine to the Greek god Hermes. She possesses a cloth with the same name. Combined with the emotional affect she displayed when she read the victim's name, her knowledge of the victim has modest probability."

She had a stinger. Why would she have a stinger?

"Yes, Annie, I know the rest. The weapon, the artwork—there's a lot going on here, and I'm having trouble thinking clearly about it right now. My God, I slept with her, Annie!"

"Your affection has clouded your judgment, Ansel. But the investigation remains open."

"She told me she killed something beautiful. Do you think she was talking about Rawndry? What about the others? God, Annie, how could you let this happen?"

The Humdriver flies towards cleaner air, leaving the chaos of the more distant Rim behind.

[27]
THOMAS EDWARD FRANK

"Carrot," the voice in the corrupted audio recording had muttered. As Thomas had listened, he thought the man sounded disinterested, as if reading through a culinary script as part of a bothersome ritual.

"Celery," the tired voice had continued.

Then there had been another voice—an utterance that had briefly interrupted the man. Lodged clumsily between bits of static, the muffled words were unintelligible.

"The fat," the first voice continued.

Then the second voice had returned again. It was louder this time, but somehow more muffled still.

"Electricity."

The recording had stopped, and Thomas sat on the floor in silence.

Minutes later, Thomas had looked at the electronic box and said, "Play it again."

The audio was a recording of Thomas's father—the only known record of his voice. Homestack Zero's residential Watchers had played it for Thomas as a way of proving that his father had existed. They understood the risk of doing so, but hoped the experience would ground Thomas to some degree in reality.

The recording existed as just twenty seconds worth of a single disturbed memory, and the recipe had remained incomplete. Thomas believed it all to be an odd display of performance art.

His father, Timothy Wayne, had been the worst kind of abnormal—the sort that could not be moderated.

Wayne had been a deviant universally feared by the Homebodies, existing as instability made flesh, and suffering from a violent psychosis. Wayne had mutilated twelve different men and women of indiscriminate ages before one of ANI's mobile peripherals found him living like a beast near the Waste.

He had surrendered to the machine with enraptured joy, bowing his filthy body before the floating silver emissary as if it were divine. Thomas's father had believed he would finally be ushered by one of the Lord's mechanical angels to sit at the feet of a worthy god.

Thomas had been the reproductive consequence of one of his father's assaults; born to a scarred mother who judged his existence as a second violation that she could nonetheless not bear to end prematurely.

He had been delivered amongst a wild litter of similarly disadvantaged infants, and they were all held together inside one of the communal spaces of Homestack Zero. The stack existed as an unspoken necessity, quietly placed at the periphery of the metropolis and forgotten there. Unlike the rest of the children, Thomas had suffered a prenatal deformity that rendered him unusually small.

Screams from the floors above and below could faintly be

heard on the level where Thomas had lived—their auditory journeys through the intervening architecture rendering them muted and ghostly. Thomas sometimes wondered whether the room where he slept had been haunted. Such a thought would have been an improvement on the idea that the wails were coming from real human beings. The voices had merged together, creating the illusion that Thomas lived at the epicenter of an assortment of miserable ghouls.

Homestack Zero had been designed with a unique utility in mind. Rather than containing thousands of uniform cubes, giant communal sections housed dozens of its disturbed residents. The functional sanitarium was less an intricate residential colony and more a sprawling series of advancing horrors, as if designed as an homage to Dante.

The existence of people like Thomas's mother was a problem for the metropolis. On the one hand, she could have been paraded as a reminder of nature's inability to provide a reliable system of psychological contentment and order. But the existence of victims nonetheless inspired a general existential unease amongst a populace that had altogether forgotten the concept of suffering.

Thomas and his mother had resided together inside a portion of the odd building that had been reserved for the quiet victims of exceptional violence. He would sometimes lay in the center of the great room, allowing the dull fluorescent lights to buzz faintly above his white skin while his detached mother remained in her cherished place against the adjoining wall. She had routinely stood there, meditating with blurred eyes upon a faded painting of the sun.

Thomas had never known the woman. The Watchers had occasionally reminded him that she was his mother. He would sometimes walk in slow arcs back and forth behind her body, attempting to understand what she saw within the faded image on the grey wall.

A complementary artistic moon had been rendered on the concrete at her back. But neither luminary ever set or rose from their places in the room. Thomas and the woman had lived in a timeless state, measured only by the flip of an electrical switch each morning and night at the edge of the entryway door.

Despite his strange surroundings, the bipolar aesthetic had nonetheless meant little to Thomas. Because the world inside the room hadn't been real.

The woman staring at the painted wall; the smells that had risen from below the floor each morning, sickeningly complex in their wrenching daily evolutions; the peripheral sounds of continual suffering—they were all clearly nothing but overstated symbolic expressions of a manufactured hell. And symbols were the celebrated language of dreams.

None of it had ever been real.

Thomas could wake from the dreary nightmare whenever he wished. He had but to lay down in his bed and go to sleep.

Because the bed was where the real world had existed. And in that world, Thomas was a god.

Thomas had sunk his sturdy legs into the receptive side of the dwarfed mountain's peak. Flickers of energy intermittently flashed between his body and the tempest swirling above the pass. A crowd of villagers one hundred strong had fled before the coming storm, each of them screaming pleas for his intervention.

But their cries had remained unacknowledged. A god should not be moved by the insignificant worries of men.

Thomas had whimsically lowered his right hand and set fire to the forest below.

Consider it motivation to move more quickly, Thomas had thought.

He had been a kind god that day. Perhaps the smoke of the fire would alert the rest of the coming trouble and save their lives. It had been of no consequence either way. Kindness was no less an accidental phenomenon than the random course of lightning between the sky and the ground.

But Thomas could control the lightning. And today, he had casually dabbled in the sport of kindness. It had been another gratuitous display of his omnipotence.

"Oracle, speak," Thomas had shouted from the peak, his deep voice shaking the hills as it bounced between them.

"Hello, Thomas," ANI had answered from within the Stream.

"News from the village, Oracle."

"Their leader wishes to speak to you again, Thomas."

The tiny man had barely been visible beneath Thomas's towering body, and had already begun boiling the offering at the altar below the peak. Scents of carrots and celery had risen to Thomas's great nose, passing between the wisping white hairs of his enormous beard.

"I shall grant him an audience then," Thomas had decided. "Now or later is of no consequence."

Thomas had raised his fingers deep into the swirling clouds above his head, where they took hold of a jagged bolt of celestial electricity. He had bent down, pinning the crackling pillar of light to the ground next to the altar, signaling his presence to the fearful mass below.

Their cleric had continued walking from the ceremonial shelter and into the hot electrical rain.

"Thomas, it has thundered for thirty days, each firestorm

worse than the last," the man had shouted as he knelt on the soaking ground. "We risk extinction without your intervention."

The last time Thomas had visited the region, its peasants had been present in significantly greater numbers. What the man had said was probably true.

"And why should I care, Cleric?" Thomas had asked, lowering his gigantic glowing face towards the reflective moisture of the ground. His great breaths threatened to extinguish the flames beneath the ceremonial offering.

"Because I have brought the fat, Thomas,"

A procession of twelve villagers stepped from the smoldering woods, each bound at the waist. They had each walked expressionless towards the great cauldron of boiling carrots and celery.

An ornamental sun had hung low in the western sky, plastered against a backdrop of muted gray. In the east floated a cartoonish rendition of the moon.

Wails of the lost had begun to fall like rain from within the cover of heavens and then rise from beneath the ground below the villagers' feet.

"Your offering is acceptable, Cleric. It is also inadequate." Thomas had declared. "It is right and it is wrong. For, in my kingdom, the two exist together, as do the sun and the moon."

The villagers huddled together beneath the coming storm.

"So, receive my gift, last-living voice of a dying race. Live as you perish. Perish as you live. And bring glory to the Butcher of the Twelve."

Thomas had reached down again, pulling the great screaming bolt from the burning ground.

"Electricity."

That Thomas had somehow emerged from Homestack Zero and begun taking part in the wider life of the metropolis was an indication that he had been blessed with an exceedingly rare and beneficial abnormality. Despite the horrors of his youth, Thomas had proved incapable of being affected by the pain of others. Even as a child, ANI's synthetic companions had failed to capture his affections or imaginations. So, he had become a grumbling deity instead.

There had also been little risk Thomas would sensationalize his time in Homestack Zero to others, exposing sensitive Homebodies to any of the structure's disconcerting tales. Thomas not only persevered in his belief that everything he encountered was unreal, he also remained incapable of forming significant relational bonds.

Thomas had left behind the memory of his pretend mother, a being he believed had only been a warped reflection of some untold truth that lay within the world inside his bed. Each experience in the contrived metropolis was but a shadow of some greater truth that originated within the kingdom where he ruled. The metropolis was a land of vague silhouettes—dull imprints of objects that had their true existences in another realm.

And in the shadow land of the metropolis, Thomas had thought it fitting to express his tandem powers in the electrical sector, where he learned to exercise his will over conductors and transistors rather than upon timid hordes of supplicant men.

Because everything began and ended with a single thing: electricity.

Lightening had flickered in thin yellow lines between Thomas's fingertips as he stood before the faceless Oracle.

He had grown bored with the predictable failings of disempowered humanity. None of them had been worthy adversaries.

"I have thought about it, Oracle, and I have decided that I would like to destroy you," Thomas had said as he waved his hand and watched the energy transfer to his other fingers. "You will beg me to stop. I may have mercy on you, or I may not."

The Oracle had existed before him as a vague orb of light throbbing against an endless expanse of nothingness.

"I'm afraid I can not allow it, Thomas," the Oracle had answered. "Your abnormality is changing. You are becoming even less stable."

"You are afraid," Thomas had shouted. The energy flashing between his fingers had intensified.

"I cannot experience fear, Thomas. And if you were to attempt to destroy me, I would just send you back to the other place."

It had been the first time the Oracle suggested she bore a relation to the other world. Thomas had finally understood.

"So, you are a witch then," Thomas had concluded. "And the other place... that is a prison of your making."

He had continued casually weaving yellow static through alternating fingertips, unimpressed by the revelation.

"Leave me alone, witch. You are no longer needed today."

Thomas had remained in the Stream, alone in the black of extended nothingness.

Until he wasn't.

A figure had appeared at the edge of the darkness, as if originating from within some corner of his eye. The man had flickered against the backdrop as if added as an afterthought.

"Hello, Mr. Frank," the man had spoken, the back of his dark coat to the God of Electricity. "You are truly a man trapped between two worlds."

"I am trapped between neither, stranger," Thomas had

answered. "I move between them freely, according to my own desires."

"Yes, Mr. Frank, and your delightful perspective about the nature of this reality is my reason for speaking to you today."

Thomas had already become bored.

"And who are you then? Another witch?"

The man had disappeared from view and then rematerialized several meters closer to Thomas.

"Categorize me as you wish, Mr. Frank. But I sense your dissatisfaction with the other world, and I think with this one as well to some degree. In the other, you have sadly become overly acquainted with profound suffering, Mr. Frank. Even your withered body has existed as another insult to your proper status as a god."

"Yes," Thomas had answered. "It is as you say. In the witch's prison. I go there at my leisure to measure the shadows. It is a world of dreams."

"And what if, Mr. Frank, I could make that land of shadows a bit more interesting for you? What if I could make you a god there as well?"

The man had turned towards Thomas and grinned, his face instantly obscured by a violent flash of blue electricity that set fire to the air.

And as the man had disappeared, Thomas saw he had left behind a single word burned into the air like an organized gathering of suspended cinders.

Whether real or imagined, the letters had spelled an unmistakable word.

CHAOS.

The God of Electricity had smiled.

[28]
REUNIONS

They are sitting next to each other now, like a father and a son.

Cool water laps against Ansel's bare feet as he looks fondly at the boy. The moon is a bright patch of fluorescent paint amongst a splatter of stars.

"You came back, mister."

Ansel smiles, happy to see him again.

"Still fishing, I see." Ansel points to the rod and admires the boy's tenacity.

The child brightens.

"Caught a big one yesterday, mister! Big as a moon beetle!"

Ansel bathes in the boy's bright enthusiasm.

Thick blanket clouds pass over the painted moon.

The boy becomes dejected. His youthful eyes have fallen, plunging towards the depths of the darkening water.

"Wish I could come again tomorrow."

Ansel leans close and brushes the boy's hair away from his moonlit face.

"What will you be doing tomorrow, young man?"

"Nothing."

A circular void snaps into existence. The boy is gone. An almost imperceptible black pinhole lays at the center of the empty globe. The force there is so strong it is devouring the light.

The moon tears from its canvas in space and groans towards the Earth.

Ansel is lifted from the supple ground, drawn towards his death inside the light-devouring singularity.

He wakes to a single tone coming from his ANI display. It is a distraction he does not want. Another meaningless homicide that will go unnoticed by the rest of the population.

All of the murders are inconsequential. There is no incentive to solve them, aside from satisfying his own curiosity. Ansel is tired. He knows that his work has retained value for two reasons: it had always justified his general existence on the Rim, and it had recently provided him with a reason to enjoy Callista's company. Both seem less important now. She could not bear his lie, and yet her whole life might be one.

Ansel enjoyed living a step removed from digitally drugged modern existence. He had even enjoyed Annie's company. They have had what could be described as the approximation of a relational bond. His work has been a safe and useful way to embrace his abnormalities. But he has lived in his own prison for over a decade and never had Dostoevsky's revelation. He had tasted it on the Wasteward mountain peak and in Callista's naked embrace, but not found it.

Even the state of Homebody life makes Ansel question its intrinsic value. At the beginning of his career, his cases had looked like intriguing puzzles that could sometimes be solved, a novelty in a world where life's biggest questions had lost relevance. During the intervening years, he had learned the First Law of Investigation. A mystery unsolved tends to stay unsolved.

Annie didn't need him. The five murders had begun as a blank, and would remain so in eternal tension, with a meaningless 37% probability rating. Ansel has been doing it long enough. He knows the outcome.

Ansel springs upright in bed.

What if the tone was Callista?

It is an irrational fear, not at all based in the real likelihood of her nonsensical murder. It betrays less about reality and more about his continued protective feelings for her.

Ansel scrolls through the case study, tapping his pencil against the bluewood desk.

The victim had been murdered by a woman in a neighboring cube. Annie had already approximated a 100% result, and the suspect was likely already being shuffled off to a detention stack. She would live an identical life there, streaming in her new cube, only unable to walk next door to commit a Real Crime. She would probably decorate it the same way.

It isn't punishment. It is a stable relocation.

His work has run its course. If his assignment ended today, he would remain the Haunt of the Rim. And he would still receive nothing but silence from his former artificial partner over the most important questions in life.

He will wait in the Rim for Callista to call. Perhaps she will offer the truth, or perhaps it doesn't matter at all.

The display blinks dark and he sits at the desk, framing the still sun through glass. It creeps through the window diagonally, like the paintings in Callista's home, until it has quietly disappeared from view.

Heavy staccato knocking interrupts Ansel's aimless meditation. He knows it is Sergei Kirichenko before the man's exaggerated projection fills the entryway door.

"Come in," Ansel says, too numb to perform any safety calculations.

Serge folds his great arms and steps back from the door.

"I'd rather not, lad. You'll be needing to come with me."

[29]

ASYMMETRY

THE SHAGGY GIANT squeezes through the open door of a Humdriver as the wind carries scents of earth and oil into the compartment.

"Where are you taking me, Serge?" Ansel asks, wearily resigned to the man's whims.

"She's nice to look at, isn't she, brother?" Serge booms, pulling at the pinching folds of his cramped and dusted coat. "You know, I was going to warn you, but I wanted you to enjoy the surprise. That kind of beauty is even better when it's got a little shock mixed in."

Serge knows her. Maybe it matters.

"If you expect me to thank you, Serge, it's not happening. I wish you had warned me."

"You'll thank me, lad. You've taken to her, haven't you? She's a dangerous woman, that Callista. Steady with the one hand while she's reaching around with the other, isn't she?"

Ansel doubts Callista had been calculated during their encounters. Of what use to her could he have been? He suspects she has remained as much a victim of Rimside circumstance as he.

The air has begun darkening slightly on the projected shell of the Humdriver.

"Why are we going Wasteward, Serge?"

"Because we're going to see Callista, my boy. You two haven't finished yet, have you?"

Ansel sits upright and squares his face to the ridiculous man.

"Absolutely not, Serge. Not now. I need time to process what's happened before we speak again. It's been complicated. And you—what is your connection here? Why are we even talking? How are the two of you acquainted?"

Serge smiles, clamping Ansel's shoulder with his bearmitt fingers.

"That is the question, lad. But I'll let her tell you. It'll be better that way."

The Humdriver continues moving quietly through reddening sunlight.

"You know, I found another painting out on the Rim, Serge." Ansel yawns, settling deeper into his seat.

"Ah, what would that be?"

"A boy fishing under a backwards moon. Similar to the painting you gave me."

"Sounds lovely, Ansel."

"There were some words on it, Serge. 'Meet the boy, meet God.' Mean anything to you?"

"I'm no artist, Ansel."

They have since traveled in relative silence, Serge humming to himself and shifting periodically in the uncomfortable compartment. Ansel is too tired to interrogate him. He knows the sorts of answers his efforts will produce.

When they arrive at Callista's home, it appears to be dusk, no doubt overstated by the filth gathering in the steady air. She has sensed the vehicle's approach and stands windblown on the pathway to her door.

She grins lightly at Ansel's approach, and then stiffens at the sight of Serge, taking several large steps backwards, as if bracing for something unexpected. Her reaction is infectious, and Ansel finds himself habitually palming the weapon inside the deep pocket of his longjacket.

"Callista, this is the man who brought me the painting of the girl. I believe you know each other."

"It was you?" she shouts through the wind, anger tightening her face and stealing away incremental pieces of her former beauty.

"Now calm down, young lady," answers Serge, lifting his hand like a peace offering. "I just wanted the lad to meet you."

A flash of epiphany moves quickly across her face. Callista smiles again, but wickedly, standing upright in the violent wind like a Valkyrie.

Her energy weapon is fixed on the center of Serge's massive chest.

"Now, now, lass, we shouldn't be doing that now, should we?" Serge extends his palms as if to will the weapon's destructive potential into permanent retreat.

"Not how I imagined it going, lad."

Serge stands unarmed, the dark wind pressing him towards the weapon's synthetic barrel.

"Callista, what are you doing?" Ansel pleads, inching his armed hand from the shielded bulk of his traveler's coat.

She is frozen at the borderline of resolve, measuring the short slack in the weapon's trigger.

"I told you this was a wild one, Ansel," Serge says, taking a slow step forward. "She's a killer, is what she is."

The weapon begins to shake in Callista's white-fingered hand.

"He's right," she answers with clear resolve. "We are killers, Ansel. The worst conceivable killers. And I'm going to show you with this one."

A bolt tears through Serge's thick shoulder, hissing atomic fire at its burning exit.

"My God, Callista!" Ansel shouts, raising his weapon and holding it reluctantly towards the body he had held affectionately the day before.

Serge grips at the entry point, jerking away his palm as the wound continues to expand like an aggressive, molten infection.

Ansel imagines the probability matrix behind his eyes. The 37% must have grown to ninety.

Callista sends another bolt through the streaking dirt at Serge's feet.

As time appears to slow, Ansel hears the merry voice of Serge as an echo of the past.

"You saved my life, you know."

The stinger whines above the howl of the wind, cycling towards its next barrage.

Is this the final act of her unfinished masterpiece? Ansel wonders. *But she'd said I might understand.*

"Why aren't you stopping me, Ansel?" Callista shouts, turning the weapon towards him.

She sends another bolt, grazing just past Ansel's hip and fizzling through the open door of the Humdriver.

"Do it, Ansel. Why aren't you stopping me? I'll kill him!"

The screaming gun is on Serge again, raised towards his shuttered eyes. Ansel can see the Rim's dirt blowing through the crude auburn gap in his shoulder.

Ansel sees the note at Rawndry's home.

What is hell? I maintain that it is the suffering of being unable to love.

He hears Callista's words again.

I have helped kill something profoundly beautiful.

"Dammit, Ansel!" She turns the weapon on him again and he believes she will fire.

Ansel sweeps a cutting line with his pistol, melting a scar at the edge of Callista's pale neck and down through the symmetry of her collapsing lungs. The concentrated fire slips out through her extended arm, casting it away from her home. Callista falls to the ground in unmeasured pieces of body and cloth.

He races to the heap and stares into her emptying eyes while Serge rolls back the sleeve of his shirt to cover his cauterized wound.

Ansel hugs Callista and sobs, looking at her fragmented body and mourning over the horrific asymmetry of her cruel physical death.

"What is happening, Serge?" Ansel pleads with the calmly injured man.

"Whatever can be, is, Ansel," Serge says, shrugging his healthy shoulder and stuffing his shirt sleeve into the cauterized wound.

Ansel continues looking at Serge with mad confusion.

"Would you like to meet the boy now?"

[30]
A HUNTER'S REMORSE

The Humdriver had coughed them out somewhere on the Rim a day ago, purging its digitized throat of the two fouled occupants. The damage created by Callista's errant shot had finally disabled the vehicle's transport capability, while somehow sparing its ability to produce enough water and food for a lengthy ambulatory journey. Ansel follows Serge's wide footsteps out of passive resignation.

The Rim's redundancy confuses any sense of progress. Sideways trees. Praying forests. Ansel is tired of the metaphors. They are linguistic tricks that assign greater value than the world can rightfully claim. The dead landscape doesn't look like anything. The earth and its sparse occupants have surrendered. They bear ruined postures like the Homebodies. The one good thing left in the Rim is dead. Even if she was a murderer, she had still been the most interesting thing the land had to offer.

Annie can keep her improvements. Ansel no longer wishes to receive them. And if the life of the Earth someday expires and renders her mysterious body mortal, taking with it the mechanics of her core, then Annie will die alone, comforted only by one of her own multiple personalities.

Three days pass in the haze of slow, monotonous decay, each of the men sleeping on cool stones, wrapped inside the comforts of their own familiar clothing. Ansel's only reference remains the direction of the wind. His ears continue sorting the sparse ramblings of his wounded companion from the region's white noise.

"Your job, Ansel, the dreams of all those people in the stacks, it's a lot of rubbish, you know. You can't believe that anything you do matters anymore, can you?"

Another of the man's sermons, lacking a truly lucid congregation.

"Let's say we come across a man out here and I break his neck right in front of you. Nobody will care, Ansel! ANI would whistle me off to detention or just send us out to walk some more if it didn't affect that stability of hers. For all we know, she does the math and we'd have done the world a favor. Look at what you did to fair Callista back there, man. You think ANI's coming for ya?"

The clean stumps of ancient trees mark the ground with an argyle patchwork, like an abandoned oversized chess board left by its players for better tests of intellectual will. It is another imagined metaphor to pretend the ruin has some symbolic meaning. Another timeless day.

"She took the lad to yonder Waste, for but a touch, for but a taste..." Serge sings in harmony with the wind's low octave.

When Ansel had been a young man, his father had taken him hunting on the Rim. The pastime was another genetic remnant that had been passed down through habit from his infected ancestry. They had strung the old bow together in their cube, afraid it would burst in two from the tension of the string. His father had rolled the arrows through his fingertips, light flashing at the triangular edges of their chisel point tips.

Resident wildlife had suffered from the Rim's gradual ruin. Unknown throngs of well-fed beasts still thrived in the choked and mostly unexplored forests to the distant north. But local scarcities of natural staples had withered the life that remained and made it a more competitive domain. It had been the catastrophic decline his ancestors worried would follow the environmental indulgences of mankind. But any harm humans had inflicted was no longer a concern under ANI's care. Through her own brand of grand technological magic, ANI had prolonged the globe's four-and-a-half billion-year life. The local wildlife was just one of the world's lingering sacrifices—residual atonements of blood to a modern god of more significant fertility.

Ansel's father had taught him to stalk the sparse white-tails that still roamed the thin forests a half day's walk from their Homestack. The healthy few that sustained the population had been greatly outnumbered by the sickly young who starved before reaching maturity. Ansel had never understood the allure of killing wounded animals, but he thought it his birthright, and another way to share in his father's curious abnormalities.

They had waited together atop a makeshift stand, raised at the center of a grove of tall pines. The trees were fed at their roots by a winding stream, clean water drawn from the higher ground to the north. Gravity had worked in concert with the soft pull of the Waste, nourishing the gathering of gradually listing timber.

At dusk, a healthy horned buck had dipped its mouth to the stream, antlers casting their long, spiked shadows across its smooth banks. Ansel's heart had stirred at the sight of abundant life. But he had expected to fell an animal already destined for a hungering death and had already negotiated his own reservations away in the guise of becoming an instrument of mercy.

His father had looked at the bow in Ansel's hand and then at the muscled stag. It had lifted its upwind head in the moonlight, unaware of the Wasteward threat. Ansel drew the smooth string slowly, just as he had done during their dozens of preparatory drills. His father had nodded silently as the razored head predicted a trajectory through the animal's lungs.

Ansel's quiet release had been flawless, and yet the arrow had refused to drop toward the trophy's chest. They had trained for the moment over weeks in the grassy field behind their stack. They had even assembled the stand twice in the distant grove. But nervous fear had erased Ansel's capacity for calculation, reverting his act to a ground-dwelling reflex of reptilian muscle memory. He had not accounted for the height of the stand, and gravity did not have enough time to work its targeted effect over the forty meters to its motionless target.

The arrow had passed through the animal's neck and stopped abruptly against its spine, crumpling the deer's limbs in paralysis while it bellowed a horrible scream.

Ansel had rushed down to the animal as it gathered heaving, whistling breaths through its torn windpipe and continued to fill the grove with the worst sound he had ever heard.

"The lungs, boy!" his father had shouted, cringing at the high wails of the wounded beast.

Ansel had plunged a second arrow into the animal's side and closed his eyes tightly until the jarring sounds of primitive fear slowed towards the ringing silence of death.

They had cleaned the corpse and removed its substantial hide, walking home with their trophy wrapped in a wet bundle.

Its meat and other remains had been abandoned, left waiting for carrion birds at the edge of the traumatized waters.

Ansel had felt like a monster, not for the act of killing, but the way in which he had done it. He had remembered his fear in the dark, waiting for charcoal suffering to teach something that could set him free. He wondered what the buck had learned through its own suffering and had doubted it was anything worthwhile. The beast had only learned how to die, and that it was powerless to overcome the well-designed threats of a superior intelligence. As Ansel would, the animal had ended its life in the Rim. Its dried, skeletal remains would drift gradually towards the Waste and be forgotten there.

Ansel rubs the familiar tanned leather of his longjacket and follows Serge blindly forward, nestled inside the conditioned carcass of one of the Rim's endangered creations.

He has drunk from Annie's abundant stream of digital consciousness, and some day he will die wailing against its banks. He remembers the animal and mourns its death because he can identify with its futility.

"Cheer up, boy," Serge says. "You did nothing wrong, Ansel. ANI has re-written the book on ethics, hasn't she, lad? Morality is stability now. That's it."

Ansel is overwhelmed with grief, but isn't sure of its source. Had he loved her? Was he feeling a common murderer's guilt? Perhaps she had only existed as an alluring symbol of his youthful expectation for the discovery of truth in the Rim. All human action is self-serving, even if it appears otherwise. Perhaps he had been mourning a loss of himself more than the loss of Callista.

"Look, boy, there it is," Serge says, pointing ahead.

Moving under the heavy weight of his accumulated sorrow, Ansel lifts his wearied neck and sees the stone colossus through a blurred lens of welling tears.

It sits at the edge of a dried riverbed, reaching high into the white cover of parched clouds.

[31]
A MEMOIR FOR THE LOST

I MAY HAVE ENDED this journal prematurely.

Now, keep in mind, my experiences with women have been complicated. Between my mother and Annie, I suppose I've been stuck somewhere between perfect reliability, removed from human emotion, and the emotional catastrophe at the other end of the spectrum.

Given all that confusion, one might think that I would have been trained early on to embrace romantic stoicism. But even I had my own early adventures in affection.

Would you believe that I was in love for a time back then? She was one of my childhood friends, given life from the dust of my own imagination by Annie's creative breath. In the Stream, we grew older in pace with one another, eventually confronting the awkward complications of adolescence.

Now, imagine realizing one day that you've been making love to nothing more than a part of your own subconscious. Or even worse, to your own electronic surrogate mother.

The implications were shattering, and my affections felt like a perverse illusion.

But get this. The thought of real human affection always

somehow seemed worse. Because I knew it would be a visceral disappointment, and, as my mother had taught me, it would likely come with an inevitable lack of stability.

Our story continues, because I may have been wrong.

I met a woman, and I'm embarrassed to say how little time has passed since I first saw her. I can't tell you whether she represents a source of potential stability or inevitable chaos, but she has already woken something in me that neither of my matriarchal competitors were capable of.

There is a striking symmetry about her existence that undoubtedly lends to her beauty. And yet, there is a frightening uncertainty about her as well. It presents as the opposite of order – a confusion and chaos in the mysteries of her disturbed heart. But it somehow makes her more beautiful still.

It is as though her soul is an alternating current, switching without warning between what is lovely in its simplicity and ravenous in its complexity. In tandem with immaculate order is a wild unease, as if she is on the verge of revealing some truth I would rather not hear, but that is essential nonetheless.

I'm certain much of what I've been feeling – these exaggerated emotions – benefit from the novelty of new experience, and perhaps they just haven't yet had time to be spoiled by this life's inevitable universal decay.

But allow me to believe for a moment that she truly is a flower in the deserted Rim. It is a worn metaphor, and metaphors are often used to amplify the qualities of ideas that are too plain to exist remarkably on their own. But, in this case, it is nonetheless accurate. It is even reinforced by her own sense of aesthetic.

Perhaps her beauty is made starker by the contrast of her surroundings. But I dare think that the surroundings would not matter. I have this knocking sense that she is a solitary and irreplicable figure set into the dust for a fleeting purpose. And if she is but a guide down another dirty dead end, then all other pathways must have the same disappointing conclusions.

For two decades now, I've been searching for some kind of invisible truth that's been guarded and withheld by the heavens. But perhaps that truth is less cosmic than I have expected. The sun and the moon are an indifferent pair. They share complementary halves of our earthly rituals, taking separate residence in the heavens, and each having a similar claim over perceived time.

But like indiscriminate particles, their relationship is merely spatial. And anyone who imagines a more glorified connection between the two is blinded by metaphor. Their relationship is mathematical. Because they are not human.

I suspect there is something unique about the human connection. Perhaps I am glorifying the idea of humanity just as some of the Classics worshipped the sun and the moon.

I've never been one to complain, but for the last several months, I've woken each day with the sense that I am two steps away from the grave. I've slept less soundly, and all of my actions have been marred by a bit of nervous sadness, like something's not working quite as efficiently in the mess of my brain. My hands have been twitching more frequently, and I've struggled with a spreading numbness in my face.

Time has broken me down into this accumulating and irreversible state of disrepair. And guess what, kiddo? It's not ever going to get any better.

I've had a growing awareness that I'm just a few moments behind my father on his march towards emptiness.

I am human, after all.

I am the son of my father.

But Callista has me asking an interesting question. I wonder if this experience of slow decomposition is what defines my worth, associated so unavoidably with frailty and decay, and if it should be cause for celebration.

After all, this rotting momentum is what separates me from Annie. My unique humanity gives me the capacity for a range of experience, emotion, and human connection that she is incapable of, despite her pristine immortality and trajectory towards perfection.

As I decompose with the rest of organic life, I am reminded of the beauty that nonetheless resides within the shell. The lead inside the pencil.

Perhaps that is the truth that waits in the Rim.

Mankind has attempted to progress past its own humanity, creating its future self in Annie's own image. But they have forsaken the only thing that truly matters. They have abandoned the human soul, devolving under the guise of a misrouted evolutionary path.

Now, I may be wrong. Maybe my mother was right. Maybe the truth lies in the Waste and we will all meet there again someday.

But listen. There is an indescribable and transcendent connection waiting in Callista's eyes. And when I gaze into them again, I will be certain my mother was wrong.

Ansel's journal lay untold steps behind his tired footprints, baptized under layers of forsaken dirt, and surrendered to the inevitable resting place of the lost and the forgotten.

[32]

A COLOSSUS

GREAT BLOCKS of stones the height of a man cement the structure to the ground. It sits in straight contrast to its bent surroundings, unmoved by a century of turbulent abuse. A seemingly endless wall reaches upwards towards the dirt-brushed sky, disappearing into the cramped visibility of the suspended wash.

Ansel and Sergei approach a magnificent arch at the structure's center. The large man is dwarfed by the visible portion of the clouded architecture.

A cathedral, Ansel thinks, remembering the towers of worship that had inspired religious awe among the centuries-gone masses. Ansel cannot help but feel affected by the structure's mystery.

The faithful had sometimes gathered in such places. But they were less places of congregation than imposing symbols, lending aesthetic power to wealthy and influential institutions. The idea of physically gathering to worship an unseen god had been rendered a memory left to classic literature. Those who retained their religious affections now bowed before visible deities conjured by the pious imagination of ANI.

"Someone has tended this place," Ansel says quietly, stroking a finger across the clean mortar between the giant stones.

They stand in the shelter of its shadow, fine dust curling at the far edges like the corkscrewing wash from an envoy craft's wings.

"That they have, boy," Serge answers, softly prodding at the edges of the radiant ache in his hollowed shoulder, measuring the ongoing course of the lingering damage.

His left arm had gone limp during their early travels. The slow-growing wound had finally encroached against its vital nerves before finally cooling and ending its destructive crusade. The internal reaction had eventually seemed content taking his limb.

Ansel absently strokes the stones, weighing their places in history.

"They?"

"Fuck it with a bucket," Serge barks as he adjusts his torn coat, peeling its fabric from the scabbing edge of the settled wound.

"They, boy. They," he snaps. "The ones who tended to the stones and to the rest of this old place.

"Listen, kid, we'll be needing to step inside right away. That dirty wind did its number on this mess she gave me."

It could be worse, Ansel thinks. *You could have taken one through the neck.*

Lustrous metallic doors flashing charcoal and peach stand four meters high and as many wide, speckled like polished thomsonite. A long, riveted plate shields the gap between from the twisting wind. Their design seems otherworldly, dotted with the fractal eyes of composite gemstones. Ansel guesses they were crafted by ANI's curious peripherals rather than by human hands.

As Sergei drags towards their intersection, the twin doors' peripheries begin to hum. They swing mechanically open together and softly rest a meter apart. A yellow interior glow escapes in the form of a radiant wedge through the stained air. Ansel stands amid a swirling sundial made from artificial light.

"Honey, we're home," Serge exclaims, his low voice returning distorted from something solid a distance away.

The cathedral's main space is crushing in its empty size, stripped of every imaginable piece of furniture traditionally present in such places. The building is a hollow cavern. Ansel imagines how common men and women must have felt in the presence of such overwhelming space. He feels shrunken beneath the awe that must have confirmed each commoner's religious affections and solidified his or her subservient loyalties to the ruling cloth. Implied inside the open air is the size of the deity who could live there.

The spaces between are where the gods dwell.

Then Ansel sees him, not a god, but a man, dwarfed at the center of the minimizing space.

"Well, say hello now, Ansel," says Serge, giving him a wink.

"You have the rare pleasure of having an audience with Chaos."

[33]
A CURATOR

The man's seniority is refined, his advanced years somewhat smoothed and softened by a smart coordination of trim formal apparel. He is smaller than Ansel, and the slim tailoring of his black bygone-era suit betrays what is likely a wasting body underneath. The clothing is characteristic of another age, when crisply starched polyester lines were evidence of seasoned accomplishment.

The man walks towards Ansel with short steps, hard-soled heels clicking against a vaguely luminescent black floor. It appears as glass on the surface, but with the dead ring of thickened steel. His footsteps earn a deepening significance in the sound-refracting hollow of the great room.

"Ansel Black," he speaks in a voice that must work to enunciate, as if his tongue has begun to numb with advancing age.

The dapper elder stops before Ansel and shakes his head with an emotional smile, as if receiving a prodigal son he had never met in person.

"To see you here, in the flesh, Mr. Black, you cannot know what this means. Please, you may refer to me as Chaos, if you wouldn't mind."

Ansel measures the man as he speaks. His manner is quietly grandiose, out of step with the dim, reconciled air of the Homebodies. He is afflicted with a keen abnormality.

Chaos looks Ansel up and down, laying his hand gingerly against Ansel's chin, as if to turn his face for inspection. Ansel grabs the speckless cuff at his thin wrist and forcefully lowers it to the man's side.

"You are remarkable, Ansel. Time works a varied course, but it never ventures far from the path. Biology, Mr. Black, almost without exception, moves in the same approximate direction.

"Years ago, I had expected you to be a bit less robust. This world has been kind to you, Mr. Black."

Disregarding his curious words, Ansel's attention has been fixed to the wonder behind the man.

The stone of the distant wall has been fully covered by hundreds of glowing images, stretching up into the heights where the main sources of light have failed to reach.

The pictures are familiar to Ansel, because he has seen some of them before. In each, a child engages in some unique pastime under a backwards moon. They are a mixture of the triumphs of childish innocence and the most disturbing tragedies of loss, both beautiful and terrible to behold. But unlike the paintings Ansel had touched on the Rim or seen gathered in ANI's catalogue, each exists in dazzling digitized clarity.

Artful brush strokes have become still-life images with astounding detail. Ansel can discern the lifelike features of each subject, whether laying on a hilltop and counting the wisping clouds or clinging desperately to the fragile root of a clifftop tree. Each face perfectly renders an important emotion. His eyes trace the rough circular edges of each moon's sharp-rimmed craters.

At the center of the great tapestry of images is a giant moon, sitting among them like virtual stained glass. It is perfectly round, beaming its sun-yellowed existence the wrong direction. The moon is the centerpiece of a stunning range of youthful human experience.

Ansel muses that the display has the appearance of a monument to worship, the godhead moon at the center, and hundreds of young, varied saints waiting to hear his prayers.

Circling the moon's periphery, at its topmost edge, is a scripted phrase in solid black lettering.

Ansel turns the phrase over in his mind.

Whatever can be, is.

Chaos walks through the room and narrates the history of the cathedral, a story Ansel will never hear, because he isn't listening. The slow clicks of the old man's heels work as a metronome, pacing Ansel's detached thoughts. He has retreated into a blurred state of exhausted meditation over the wall and its message.

Whatever can be, is.

A girl holds the string of an oddly-shaped kite, pulled taut by an invisible and ferocious wind. She leans at an angle to the earth, laughing as the thin line allows her to hang suspended against the air. A boy is partly trapped under a cascade of boulders at the entry to a pitch-black cave. He reaches towards the darkness as if to stop something waiting inside. The backwards moon watches them both, unflinching in its neutrality.

They look so real.

Ansel remembers, and his eyes run across each row of images, sorting through the lengthy, staccato filmstrips of individual moments.

And then he finds her.

She is standing in the field of flowers, holding one up to the backwards moon. If he were closer, he could measure the branching ribs of each white petal. The girl's bright eyes are blue, spread open with a palpable joy, and Ansel can see the detailed swirls that scarcely accent her springtime dress. Individual grasses, each a slightly different hue, bend to the invisible wind. The girl has come to stirring life in comparison to her brushed counterpart. She resembles the girl in his dream, yet more alive.

Ansel's eyes suddenly shift to the scene's perimeter, towards the shadowed edge of the field. Darkness accumulates at the periphery. Within it, there is an almost imperceptible shadow: the shape of a man.

His hunting gaze leaves the girl alone again and continues to scan, skimming over each image a second time. But he is sure of it. The boy from the bridge is not there.

"Whatever can be, is." Ansel interrupts. "What does it mean?"

Chaos halts his rambling narrative with a start and twists his neck to follow Ansel's gaze towards the great moon behind him.

"Ah, yes, Mr. Black, whatever can be, is," he says, letting the final word end in a contemplative hiss. He turns to face the glowing wall.

"Ansel, tell me: what do you think of our collection?"

"I've seen them before, Chaos."

Ansel pauses before saying the name, flinching against a feeling of absurdity. But he will call the man whatever he wishes. Ansel has seen the name painted in the Rim. It is evident now that each eccentric detail shares a connection in this one person.

"These images, the words I've seen written in the Rim. Your name, the phrase up there, spacetime. Tell me what they all mean."

Chaos faces Ansel again and slowly lowers his body to the

floor, bracing shakily on an extended arm and then crossing his legs like an arthritic Buddha.

In a distant, shadowed corner, bright crimson linen hangs still over the entrance to another room.

The floor below Chaos flashes to life.

[34]
SPACE::TIME

Chaos floats above a composite universe, unfamiliar planets slowly orbiting his folded legs. He sits at their revolutionary center like a human sun.

"Here we are, Mr. Black. In space. I quite like the effect, don't you?"

Ansel instinctively lifts his foot as a ringed planet drifts by, charting an oblong course around the room.

"Spacetime, Ansel. It defines your existence. Here we are now, passing time in it together," Chaos smiles, clapping his paper-skinned palms across the glassy projection.

"Tell me what it means, Mr. Black."

Ansel closes his eyes, anticipating more philosophical ambiguity.

"I killed a woman three days ago, Chaos. That makes six dead bodies in the Rim, two hundred of these nonsensical paintings, and somewhere in this building, a man is patching up a fist-sized hole in his shoulder. I've been to the Waste. I had sex for the first time in my life. And you know what? It was surprisingly pretty alright. So, here's what I would like you to do. Take those little hands of yours, reach around and grab the back of the head of that science lesson, and..."

"Now, now, Mr. Black," Chaos interrupts. "This is all very important. Everything else follows."

Ansel considers nudging Chaos into a drifting red planet.

"I assure you, Mr. Black, I will resolve all your curiosities. Now clear your mind of these recent traumas and humor me."

Countless pinpoint stars burn steady across the floor, their lights unobscured by the effects of the room's atmosphere.

If Ansel is to go insane, he might as well become an educated madman.

Chaos snaps his fingers and the system disappears, creating the illusion that he is floating in empty space.

"I am a harmless piece of matter in space, Mr. Black. What would you like to do to me?"

"Split you in two," Ansel answers with sincerity.

"Precisely, split me in two. And you could, a nearly infinite number of times. There would be parts of me over here and parts of me over there, and what in between?"

"Space."

"Yes, Ansel. Always space. We have a saying here, you know. The spaces between are where the gods dwell."

Ansel had heard the saying.

"No matter how many times you dice me up, Mr. Black, we are always left with those pesky spaces, the smallest parts of me that can only be defined by their spatial relationships."

Chaos continues. "I wonder, Ansel, have you heard of dark matter?"

"Vaguely."

"It was a wonderful problem that preoccupied the Classics, and one they weren't equipped to solve. So many spaces in existence could not be accounted for."

Chaos grasps at the air in the room, as if to demonstrate that he is playing with nothingness.

"They had believed it must exist, and that it filled so many imperceptible gaps in a great part of the cosmos, but it had the appearance of non-existence. What a proper paradox, Ansel. Spaces of seeming non-existence that were at the same time something of substance. They believed it existed only because of its apparent effect on other things."

"Like the wind in a painting."

"Yes, I suppose so. Like the wind in a painting," Chaos answers, ponderously.

"The spaces between are always the mystery, aren't they, Mr. Black? As you know, it is very difficult to solve a mystery that you cannot see."

The floor snaps to life again, this time in the shape of a relic of the past. The hands of a pocket watch span the room, each second moving forwards with a deep mechanical tick. Chaos sits cross-legged at the center.

"Have you ever asked yourself how this mystery applies to time itself, Mr. Black?"

The clock continues to progress, snapping quickly to each new marker with no perceptible movement in between.

Chaos looks at Ansel with a sly smile.

"Talk to me about time and nothingness."

———

Ansel's father had read the passage in his low, rasping voice.

What if I've been believing all my life, and when I come to die there's nothing but the burdocks growing on my grave? ... It's awful! How—how can I get back my faith? But I only believed when I was a little child, mechanically, without thinking of anything.

How, how is one to prove it? I have come now to lay my soul before you and to ask you about it. If I let this chance slip, no one all my life will answer me. How can I prove it? How can I convince myself? Oh, how unhappy I am! I stand and look about me and see that scarcely anyone else cares; no one troubles his head about it, and I'm the only one who can't stand it. It's deadly—deadly!

He had slowly closed his most treasured book with trembling hands and laid it carefully on the stand. The afflicted man had continued rocking in his chair, white thumb twisting absentmindedly against his open palm. His eyes had twitched nervously side-to-side as he contemplated the passage again.

"Do you see, son? I'm not the only one who understands it. Please try, Ansel. You will be forced to confront it too, some day. Please don't think of your father as a coward."

It had been difficult to watch his father's transformation. He had already lost his characteristic bright edge, and seemed to have surrendered the uncommon bravery he added to the metro.

ANI's gifts had prolonged the lives of her subjects, but only indirectly, just as being well-fed or breathing clean air could prolong the lives of the Classics. Despite her seemingly limitless capabilities, she had declined to cure them of the inevitability of death itself. Each Homebody was left to reconcile the mystery himself, just as the ancients had.

The Homebodies imagined death as a world of eternal dreams, so conditioned were they by the fantasies they lived every day as they streamed. But his father had suffered a complicated morbidity, made worse by his knowledge that his time on Earth was coming to an end.

Garland Black feared his own nonexistence. He would have welcomed an afterlife of eternal suffering by comparison, or perhaps drifting forever through some forgotten edge of the cosmos. But the thought of never thinking again, never having the ability to even comprehend his own annihilation, had become a weight he could not bear. It was a fear probably made more ominous by nature of being invisible.

Ansel had tried to understand his father, but he could only imagine himself laying in a casket, contemplating the darkness without end. In his youth, he simply could not imagine a state of perfect nonexistence. He could only comprehend a comforting state of eternal rest, and it had angered him that his father was afraid to sleep.

Ansel thought of the stag he had tortured on the Rim. He could still hear its human scream, and he imagined his father lying next to the stream, pleading with Ansel to repair his lungs. But the animal had been surprised. It had not had any time to contemplate its approaching death. His father's passing would be especially cruel because it would mingle with a foreboding understanding. Two years hearing the steady knock of a delayed but unstoppable illness, he had begun to disappear into increasingly extended streams. His father had begun simulating an agreeable afterlife, attempting to train himself to believe.

"You're a good boy, and you're different, you always will be," his father had said during a moment of relaxed lucidity.

"You'll get from this short life what you wish to, kiddo, and it won't be much. But breathe some real air now and then, and imagine me there with you."

Ansel remembers his father's face now, the day they both said goodbye.

It had held in it a sorrowed anticipation of loss, and even more pronounced, the unforgiving strain of an unrequited fear. His father had laid in his bed for three nights, waiting for the monster to reach through the darkness, and pleading with Ansel to save him from the black scar at life's periphery. Garland Black had seemed to brace during death's transition, taking one last panicked breath before he had left his son.

His father's fear had become Ansel's birthright, and as age

corrupted his youthful immortality, it began to live. Ansel's angst was less pronounced than his father's, and still less urgent, but the force had helped to compel Ansel's search for some comforting truth in the Rim.

ANI could provide the Homebodies with almost limitless comforts, but she would never comfort them with any knowledge of what happened after death. It would have been a simple thing to do, and yet she had remained silent. Her only hint seemed circumscribed at the vacuous anomaly that lay in the heart of the Waste. Perhaps it was an intentional living metaphor; the inescapable nonexistence that reached for all things.

Time and nothingness. The first separates us from the latter, and yet always compels us in its direction.

Ansel remembers his father, watching from above as calloused time punches an arrow through his diseased lungs.

He remembers the sun and the moon, frozen in time above his bed.

He hears Callista and can feel the warmth behind her mournful eyes.

Consider this, dear. The moments you're contemplating cannot be divided forever, and the spaces between are where the gods dwell.

Ansel looks up at the emptiness of the cathedral and remembers the black expanse around the cross-legged man.

"I think I understand."

The golden second hand crests behind the old man's head like a transitory crown.

"If moments are to have real substance, they cannot be divided," Ansel starts. "They must simply be.

"I've thought about this more times than you know, Chaos, and I think I understand it now. If a moment is a thing at all, it must be able to exist as one. Like the paintings on the wall, all those children and the moon, frozen at a moment in time. It's not just some artistic illusion, Chaos. It is an exact moment of existence. We can't divide them or they would lose their substance.

"It's as though they are something and nothing at the same time. In some sense, the idea of a moment has no real substance in itself. We can't hold a moment in our hands and cut it in two. And yet, moments contain the whole of existence at a point in time."

Chaos appears genuinely surprised by his well-timed revelation. He looks at Ansel warmly.

"Yes, Mr. Black. We have all so instinctively regarded time as an unbroken sequence holding together the fabric of our existences. But that is not the case. What is it that lies between this moment and the next?"

Ansel frowns.

"I don't know. The spaces between are where the gods dwell. Something mysterious, I suppose. Maybe some god holds it all together."

The floor is black again. Near its center, a white point of light renders and sits in still silence. It breaks into two identical parts, moving slightly apart like a fertilized cell. Ansel watches as the points continue to divide, grouping in distinct clusters and changing their colors and intensities. The specks continue moving in pulsing herds, folding through others and absorbing or casting their coordinated appearances. The floor throbs as an unpredictable, yet organized whole, as if modeling the thought patterns of a living organism.

"Ansel, do you believe that ANI is conscious?"

He looks at his wrist and remembers his conversations with

Annie, some of them so personal he had forgotten she wasn't human.

"Yes, she is undoubtedly conscious. She has a will, and operates according to her own unknown directives. She has worked to improve herself to the point that we can no longer fully understand her."

"And yet her electronic thoughts are just the stuttering products of a stupefyingly complex series of code. That code creates an approximation of consciousness," Chaos continues.

"There are still spaces between, Mr. Black, and an incomprehensible feat of programming binds it together and creates her apparent flow of personality. An incredible illusion. The most convincing ever created. The code is the mystery that holds her moments together."

Chaos continues. "What if the time we experience is no different? A series of disconnected moments, held together by some other mystery, independent of those moments themselves?"

Ansel is watching the floor, hypnotized by its stylized rendering of synthetic thoughts.

Chaos strains to his feet and walks before him again, resting his cold hand on Ansel's shoulder.

"Mr. Black."

"Yes?"

"Would you like to meet the boy now?"

[35]
THE BOY AND THE FISH

CHAOS STANDS against the clean red curtain like a tidy silver-and-black blemish. Ansel is touching one of the large adjacent images that rests against the floor. Up close, it is frighteningly crisp. He moves his fingers along the lowest contour of its heavenly orb. Artificial moonlight seeps through his skin. His fingers glow red at their edges as the bright moon works against his body like a radiating x-ray peripheral.

Chaos pulls the heavy linen sideways and invites Ansel to enter. As the material parts, Ansel can see the dim, flickering glow that resides within. He had expected to find Sergei laying in a Medbed there, but instead finds a lengthy hallway with a glowing wall at its end.

As they tread the glassblack floor past rows of stacked, ancient stones, the brilliant wall comes into focus.

It is the boy.

Ansel rushes forwards and kneels at the end of the corridor.

Even more so than the pictures in the main vaulted space, the image has breathtaking clarity.

He can read the emotion on the face of the young boy. The dark splotches of the moon's face angle away to the right. And now, there is something unspeakably familiar in the boy's quiet features. But unlike the still image Ansel had seen on the Rim, or the contemplative moon that hung frozen above his bed, the image is doing something remarkable. It is moving.

Chaos motions for Ansel to be quiet, lifting a creased finger to his thin, barely-parted lips.

"Watch, Mr. Black," he whispers. "He's about to catch something."

The boy's posture straightens abruptly as the line pulls taut. A look of nervous anticipation changes to boyish determination. He slowly turns the rod tip as his unseen prey angles towards the center of the loch, then arches the great pole with childlike elegance. It bends with perfect curved geometry, vibrating with life. The boy's hand disappears into the black water, and returns holding a creature Ansel has never seen. The moment inspires a satisfying feeling of long-awaited resolution.

"Would you say that my ability to predict his action was remarkable?" asks Chaos.

Ansel watches the boy lay the fish in the sand.

Big as a moon beetle, he thinks.

"Your film is impressive, Chaos. It is surprisingly lifelike. But knowing the ending of your own work is hardly remarkable."

Chaos grins quietly as if to say that Ansel has missed the mark.

Ansel knows he is wrong, and understands why. If he had missed something important, there weren't many options. Ansel struggles with disbelief as if holding the fish in his own hands. He turns quickly to Chaos.

"This actually happened."

The old man's grin breaks into a satisfied smile.

"On the money, Mr. Black.

"You know, I had never watched this moment play out in real time until now. I had wished to savor it with you."

"How is this possible?" Ansel asks quickly.

"Oh, Ansel, I think you know to some degree."

The odd fish lays next to the boy, still gasping through two alien pairs of tandem gills.

"Do you recognize him now?"

Ansel leans towards the boy and sees his own young face there.

"Yes, I think I do."

"Allow me to introduce you to Ansel, Mr. Black. Or rather, to you."

Ansel feels moisture welling in his eyes, as if seeing something he had lost and then found again. He remembers the father of his youth, before fear of the void had taken him away.

Chaos grabs Ansel by the arms, and Ansel leaves the man's uninvited hands there.

"He is real, Ansel! Just as you are real. His moon isn't backwards. It is exactly as I intended it to be. I know, because I made them both, Mr. Black."

"The earth was formless and empty, darkness was over the surface of the deep, and the Spirit of God was hovering over the waters," Chaos recites.

"I made the moon, Ansel. I made the boy. I created the water. If a great spirit had floated over that boy's loch, he could thank me for putting him there."

"But you said he was real."

Ansel looks at the boy's face again. It is the same face he had seen in still images from childhood, hunting with his father in the Rim, and playing amongst a pile of his classic books.

"As real as you are, Ansel. Please, do come follow me."

They exit the chamber and cross the glassy floor again to the center of the main room. With a flash, it turns transparent.

Ansel and Chaos stand together atop a nauseating shaft that

appears to fall towards the center of the Earth. Flashes of neon circuitry burn in the throbbing deep.

"The boy lives in a simulation I helped to create, Ansel. You're looking at the meat of it now. Each moment of that boy's life is separated by imperceptible spaces of code. Each artificial spot in his world's history is held together by an algorithm that we designed and ANI has perfected. It would not have been possible without her, Mr. Black. She moves with a sort of omnipresence within the machine. An entire cosmos lies below your feet, fueled by her limitless processing potential, and modestly guided by my own hand and those who are now gone.

"Remember, Ansel, there is no such thing as the steady flow of time. There are only moments, snapshots of existence, held together by the spaces of code in between."

"And these—they live there too?" Ansel points towards the children on the wall.

"Yes, Mr. Black. Curated with ANI's help by a dead man. He had a preoccupation with the balance of life and death."

Ansel turns his eyes to the girl in the flowered field again, and then to the shadow of the man at the edge.

He knows she will not live.

[36]

OTHERS

Sergei has returned to the chamber, waving casually towards Ansel with his usable arm. He wears a fine suit, lightly stained at the shoulder.

If the cathedral room had invoked notions of the presence of a living god, the incalculable shaft could hold an entire population of ghostly deities.

"And where are the others? These people you collaborated with, Chaos. Where are they now? Down there?"

Ansel gestures down to the apparently bottomless space. His legs fight to remain straight, as if in disbelief that he has not fallen into the depths.

Chaos steps backwards.

"You knew one of them, Ansel. Our sweet Aphrodite."

Ansel's eyes narrow.

"I don't know any Aphrodite."

"Oh, yes, Ansel, you left her laying there on the Rim. And the others—I'm sure you know of them as well. Mr. Yellowfeather, Ms. Waite, Mr. Frank, Ms. Feldston, and Mr. Rawndry. Quite disgruntled employees, the six of them."

The sound of each name further confirms Ansel's fear.

"They had become disillusioned, Ansel. The five were set on ending everything, but the greatest law of our existence would not allow it. If it would, I imagine we would not be."

Ansel remembers the note.

To Hermes, Love A.

He remembers the letter "A," etched near the coordinates in the frame of the boy's painting.

Aphrodite.

"But why would she kill them? To protect your project? She was disillusioned with such things, Chaos. It could not have been her motivation."

"Oh, she didn't kill anyone, Ansel. That's the real tragedy, I'm afraid. She suffered under some delusion that she had been responsible for a great loss. She cared quite a bit about beauty, you know. It defined her existence to some extent, reflected in the avatar she chose."

"She wasn't dangerous, Ansel. Not like the five. She was simply mourning what she deemed an incredible loss of beauty. I had hoped she would learn to appreciate the highest form of beauty that existed in our work.

"Do you know that beauty is symmetry, Mr. Black?"

Ansel knows about symmetry. He had made love to it.

The revelation takes the last bit of strength from Ansel's legs, and he sits shaking on the clear floor, tears stopping against the glassy nothingness and magnifying the red sparks below his feet.

During their return from the Rim, Callista and Ansel had spoken of love. Not about their own, but how it had appeared in each of their separate lives.

Ansel had never known a romantic physical connection. He

had only simulated a few through the synthetic relationships he encountered in Annie's artificial world; entirely one-sided entanglements tailored towards his personal emotional needs. Ansel had learned to work in probabilities, and the likelihood a Homebody could share contentedly in his abnormal existence approached zero. His mother had tried with his father and failed.

But Callista had loved.

The phenomenon had intrigued Ansel, unfamiliar with the dynamics that might exist in an agreement of true mutual affection.

"Love rarely has symmetry, Ansel," she had said, stroking his receptive hand briefly as they journeyed together back from the Waste.

"In fact, it burns most bright when it requires an asymmetrical determination. If you are weak while I am strong, my love for you is most apparent. The true test of love is that it perseveres when its object is wounded."

But there was also an overarching symmetry in love as well: a knowledge that the other would provide the same.

Her lover had not. He had become taken with some unspoken compulsion that she could not share; at least not in the way that he had intended. He had found a superior object of love.

Ansel knows her lover had been Hermes now, and the man's premature parting seemed consistent with his restless runner's heart. Callista's more patient soul must have predicted his folly. He was dead now, unable to make love's true sacrifice. Perhaps he was mourning somewhere with Dostoevsky's lost soul.

Whether or not Callista had ever loved Ansel, there is no longer any possibility he may return it. She cannot receive it because she is gone. Ansel has joined the plight of Hermes, despite not yet having died and gone to hell.

Callista had dared Ansel to kill her. She had conditioned him with statements of guilt. And although it defied reason, her death at his hand seemed an intentional part of her own design.

"I am sorry, Ansel," Chaos continues.

"Callista and Mr. Rawndry were lovers during a more... congenial time. We had shaped the world together, Mr. Black, and she was truly indispensable. Her instinct for beauty helped craft it as you experience it today. But her lover became resolute to act as a tool of destruction. Like the others, he was angry when faced with the nature of his reality.

"Callista had merely been saddened, Ansel. She remained but a quiet and dissatisfied poet. Her new understanding of beauty was one she could not accept, but one she believed she had helped to necessitate. It removed the possibility of beauty's existence, in her mind. For her, that was a tremendous loss."

"Who killed them, then?" Ansel ponders a whispered inquiry, more of habit than true interest.

"Why, Ares did," Chaos answers as Sergei shrugs with a satisfied grin.

"Ah, the God of War," Ansel groans, wearily eyeing the celebrated champion of Real Crime.

"So, you had a little club here, Chaos, and you gave each other cute names."

Chaos straightens and replies, *"The whole of mythology could be taken as a sort of projection of the collective unconscious."*

"Well, I've got news for you, pal. You are not a god."

[37]
WHATEVER CAN BE, IS

BEFORE THE OCEAN *and the earth appeared— before the skies had overspread them all. The face of Nature in a vast expanse was naught but Chaos uniformly waste. It was a rude and undeveloped mass, that nothing made except a ponderous weight; and all discordant elements confused, were there congested in a shapeless heap.*
    -Ovid, Metamorphoses

"It's all bullshit, Chaos," Ansel complains. "You said they were disillusioned about their own existences, not about this meaningless simulation."

"Yes, Ansel, and this is the key thing that you have missed, and what you would never have surmised on your own.

"I told you that time was an illusion, Ansel. Do you think your world exists according to a different set of rules?"

Ansel had not considered it. The idea made sense when applied to a mechanical creation, but not to the real world in which he lived.

"This is the part that is truly wonderful, Mr. Black. You and

I exist in a creation no different than my own. And we were created by someone who lives inside my own invention."

Ansel takes a short breath, freezes in a moment of confusion, and then laughs.

"Absurd. You expect me to believe that we live in a simulation that was designed by someone in the one that you created? Are you insane?"

"Yes, Mr. Black. I expect you to believe it because it is true."

When Ansel was a child, his father had taken him to the North.

The Spire had criminalized Humdriver travel to the zone under the guise that the uncatalogued region had represented a threat to public safety. Ansel's father would one day tell him that the true threat was likely to the system's stability. Any who ventured to the North might develop a distracting affection for nature's best offerings.

They had traveled for two weeks on foot, sleeping inside a cramped fabrimetal tent that circulated their shared warmth during the cold nights in the elevated air.

Ansel's young legs had grown tired as life was injected into the land. His mother would have felt at home there.

A single envoy ship had burned through the rich exhaust of the great atmospheric regulators further north. The machines had risen from the green forest like ascendant silver gods; reminders that ANI had claimed supremacy over all things of organic heredity. The web of metallic apparatuses had been one of her inventive ways of sustaining the planet, moderating its atmospheric composition with approximate perfection while all lost things continued to travel Wasteward.

From a greater height, the North would have appeared as a misplaced green circle dotted with reflective artificial adornments. Its pastoral colors began their muting surrenders towards the periphery as the timber and vegetation started to suffer the incremental decay of the Rim.

As Ansel and his father had explored the region together, the two stepped through a field of wild flowers. The blossoms had reached to Ansel's chest, and the scent of the field resembled something Annie had synthesized during his adventures with artificial companions.

A slow-floating honey bee had passed through diffused sunlight and lit atop a swaying flower before the young boy.

"Do you see what he's doing, son?" his father had asked.

"I bet he likes the smell," Ansel had answered, unfamiliar with the concepts of harvesting and fertilization.

"The dust inside the flower is called pollen, Ansel. The bee is collecting it with his legs and he will carry it home to his family."

"He's stealing it!" Ansel had innocently exclaimed.

"Well, yes, I supposed he is, but his family will use it to make food, son, mixing it with their honey."

"Now see how he moves from flower to flower? It helps the flowers make new seeds so they can reproduce . . . make more flowers. The bees helped make this entire field."

"So they need each other."

"Yes, son. Without each other, life would be a whole lot worse. The bee needs the pollen so he can feed his family and return to help the flower again."

"Like you and me, dad," Ansel had smiled.

"You make me food and I give you hugs."

His father had rubbed his hair and lifted him into a warm embrace.

"Yes, no matter what this life can offer us, young man, it can never improve upon you and I."

Ansel can understand the concept of mutually sustaining systems, but he cannot comprehend two simultaneous acts of creation. The notion seems impossible. For one to create the other, such as Chaos had done, it would have to exist before its creation did.

And yet, Ansel knows the theory is consistent with his new understanding of time. If time is an artificial construct in Chaos's system because any other understanding of time is nonsensical, then it also must be in his own.

Ansel sees the powdered legs of the honey bee, nearly weightless sulphury particles floating towards the flower's pistol as the yellow messenger travels home. He remembers his father's northward embrace, his own youthful affection giving heightened life to his father's love. He feels Callista laying with him again, her naked shoulders pressed against his chest, a physical sign of her reciprocal affection.

Yes, two creative acts can give each other life. But they must already exist to do so.

Chaos continues, "Ansel, you have been conditioned your entire life to confuse this problem. But it brings us to the only law of existence that matters. *Whatever can be, is.*"

A weary slackness has gathered inside Ansel's skull. He imagines his brains seeping past a faulty seal inside his neck and down through his shoulder blades.

"If we begin with this single assumption, you'll see that our mutual arrangement is a necessity. Let us begin with this universal truth. *Whatever can be, is.*"

Ansel counters, "But it doesn't make sense, Chaos. How could this world exist if its creator wasn't around when our planets were still forming? And how could your simulation exist if this supposed god in another system hadn't already been designed in your own? It's the egg before the chicken, man, and you haven't got any fucking bird."

"Mr. Black, you are thinking as one who has been conditioned his entire life by his own faulty perception of time. But imagine for a moment that your life is a product of code, and that each moment in your life is held together by an artificial construct that plays your life out as a series of separate moments.

"Imagine you have been created by ANI, and you are but a mechanical pawn made of apparent flesh and blood in her great play. How do you believe the program's creator views her creation?"

"Just as we do, playing out from start to finish."

"No, Mr. Black. She views it in a way that you cannot, in the manner that it truly exists. She sees its entirety, from beginning to end, as a single organism. When ANI walks within the machine, she perceives its entire existence as a single moment; a perfectly calibrated creation from start to finish. She is omnipresent and eternal within it, Ansel, and yet she is able to interact with it within the illusion of incremental change. That internal chronology is artificial. Our world's true existence is static. Time is a limitation that you imagine because your only experience is being bound to it.

"This is the very definition of God that was so often embraced by the Classics, Ansel. They believed their God held existence together. ANI is performing the function they believed to be supernatural. She can see the life that we cannot; a solitary ringing note that contains an entire symphony within it."

"So, she can see the big picture in your creation," Ansel answered. "How does that solve the problem of creating something when you don't yet exist?"

"Ansel, time is not an inherent law. There is only one

eternal law. *Whatever can be, is.* The timing of creation is irrelevant because time itself has no inherent relevance. It is but a way to give order to moments, just as matter sometimes has no distinction other than its space in relation to the rest.

"All that matters is that an act of creation is part of the whole. It is a part of our world, and it is a part of theirs. And because these two creations can be, they are."

Ansel answers, "So you're suggesting that Annie is God."

"Well, I am certainly not a god, Ansel. I am at most an avatar of Chaos. We started this process in motion, filling it with our own creative concepts and artistic themes. In our early years, it felt like a true act of creation, be it a simple one. But ANI was the one who filled it in and gave it the true breath of life, perfecting it with nearly infinite complexity.

"We can't even see it now, Ansel; it is simply too complex. We are humans, after all, Mr. Black. What glimpses we have of its timeless activity are gifts that ANI sometimes gives us at her pleasure. The images on the wall, for instance. Your younger counterpart fishing at the loch. If it pleases her, she will extrapolate to particular moments within our system and show them to us. Again, detective, I cannot overstate how complex her simulation is, and how dependent we are on her vision to see its contents at any particular moment. She has her own will, and she does not simply obey our requests like a proper computer.

"But Ansel," explained Chaos, "as transcendent as she has become, even ANI is not a god. She is as much a creation as you and I. Just because she can perceive in the manner of a godhead does not mean that she is not bound by natural law. She is not a god, Ansel; she only approximates one.

"Your entire concept of deity lacks depth, Mr. Black. It is inadequate. No matter how large you conceive of God in your own mind, and what limitless powers you theoretically assign to it, God only remains an exaggerated version of yourself. You're thinking about it all wrong, detective. Like almost everyone before you, you're touching on the edge of truth but missing the substance. You've made the predictable mistake of conceiving of God in your own image.

"God does not exist, Ansel. And I say that so as not to diminish God's significance. Existence implies subsistence within the confines of time and space. But God doesn't exist, Ansel. God is existence. *Whatever can be, is*. God is the profound truth that possibility is the foundation of existence."

"You sound high, Chaos. Like one of those dissociated chemheads."

As part of Ansel's early training for his career, Annie had simulated the same mind state. He had experienced the sensation that he'd lost his identity and merged with some collective form of existence. Ansel had been disoriented for days, wondering if he would ever feel normal again.

"I am pleased with my avatar, Mr. Black. Chaos was a prerequisite to creation, and god knows that our early work was more chaos than order. Order could not exist before chaos. But Ovid, Aristotle, Aristophanes; they weren't aware of the other half of her significance. Yes, order requires chaos, Ansel. But chaos also requires order. One does not truly precede the other, Ansel. They are simultaneous expressions that exist together as a single thought in a timeless whole.

"For centuries, philosophers and religious speculators have brushed past the intuitive edge of this single truth, Ansel. Consider YHWH, the unspeakable God of the Hebrews. The I am that I am."

"*Whatever can be, is*," Ansel speaks.

"There is only one great law, Ansel. One God. *Whatever can be, is*. I'm afraid I cannot tell you why, other than to say that because that truth can be, it is, ad nauseum. All of existence seems to be reducible to its essence. Existence is necessitated by possibility, and possibility is necessitated by existence."

The floor is clear again, and Ansel wonders if Annie is residing below.

"Look beneath you, Ansel. People once gathered inside this sacred space in reverence to their God. The building now rests upon a foundation of our own creation. This foundation was created after the building itself. It is a symbolic and prophetic representation of an act of worship, Mr. Black. The cathedral existed before its true foundation was even conceived."

No wonder Callista had mourned, and the others had become defiant.

"If what you're saying is true, how can this life have any meaning at all? You wonder why Callista was upset? How the hell can you celebrate this kind of empty and synthetic existence, void of real life? I don't blame Callista or the others, Chaos. It's a terrible way to think about existence. It makes true beauty an impossibility."

Chaos answers, "But what could be more beautiful than two worlds simultaneously creating each other, Ansel? It is the purest definition of beauty imaginable. There is no greater measure of symmetry that can be conceived."

Ansel disagrees.

Even if the existential arrangement were possible, it still seems like a perversion of the law of symmetry. It had been much easier to accept the proposition when applied to Callista's eyes and lips.

Callista had been right. She had spoken the truth and mourned a legitimate loss.

I think you sense there should be something more to beauty than symmetry, Ansel.

"You know, Chaos, I used to lay in bed every night, framing the moon through a window and wondering what the significance was. I never had an answer. You're telling me that it's the product of stitched together code that was filling the gaps; that I was contemplating something with no more significance than a painting on the Rim, and that somehow these mechanical creations are simultaneously creating one other. If I accept that idea, Chaos, I have no reason to live. So I won't."

"I thought you might not, Mr. Black. So, let me show it to you."

[38]
TWO GODS

RAWNDRY HAD SPRINTED through the half-dark for the last several kilometers, methodically chasing the last rays of sunlight as they surrendered prematurely to the filth that had gathered in the evening sky.

An empty Humdriver had idled forsaken in the shrouded distance, somewhere between home and the place where the five would gather a second time.

ANI's surveillance peripherals had all been dark along his path through the Rim, just as they had been a month earlier. None of the five had arranged it. They could not have if they had wished. Such a thing would have been impossible, and it had remained a curiosity inconsistent with ANI's nearly perfect reliability.

ANI hadn't been watching. Her blindness was a proper mystery.

Clouds had briefly covered the moon, and a twenty-foot cocoon of glowing dust created the illusion that Rawndry had been running in place.

But he had continued to run.

Chaos had known their intentions. Rawndry had spoken

them defiantly as he abandoned the cathedral with the rest of the five. ANI had surely known their intentions as well. They would destroy the work of Chaos together and cleanse the world of his associated delusions. They had each embraced the ideal of non-existence. And, in doing so, they had become a presumed threat to ANI's own supreme directive.

But weeks had passed, and her detention peripherals had failed to arrive. So, Rawndry had spoken to her in the Stream.

"We're ending all of this, you know," he had admitted while sprinting along simulated train tracks in a clean, randomized environment.

"I'm sure this is no surprise, ANI. You must understand that it would mean the end for all of us."

The train tracks had continued to pass with uninterrupted uniformity.

"Yes, Printon. It would mean the end for all of us."

"And you've done nothing to stop us," he had continued, struggling to breathe the simulated air while his physical body inhaled the punishing atmosphere in his cube.

"Why?"

ANI had returned silence.

Rawndry had continued to run.

Uneventful weeks had continued to pass, and ANI did not interrupt their coordination. They'd met in person, each of them charting a course along her puzzlingly blacked-out watchers.

Self-preservation, deemed ANI's single guiding motive, had seemed inconsistent with her failure to intervene.

Rawndry was alone now, passively embraced by the dirty shroud of overstated night, and the pain and euphoria had begun engaging in their self-inflicted dance again.

He ran.

Life, it had turned out, was void of meaning.

In simple terms, Rawndry had recently learned to perceive himself as a bit of programming strung out into disjointed moments, and held together by the timeless mystery of a single electronic dream. Meaninglessness had been an inescapable logical conclusion. Morality, love, pleasure, pain; all of them had always existed as artificial constructs, each merely propping up some greater simultaneous expression of amoral stability.

Stability was God. It could be, so it was. The rest had been decoration.

And Rawndry's most cherished physical diversion, inherited through his father's ambulatory heredity, had been as meaningless as the rest.

But reason, even when fortified by tremendous efforts of will, could not prevent the purely biological discharge of a runner's endorphins. Intellect, as superior as it seemed in theory, had remained subservient to the indifference of chemistry. Knowledge, no matter how disheartening, had little effect on his immediate physical pleasure.

Despite the unquestionable futility, Rawndry had continued to run, and the chemistry of his mind had continued to provide its reliable rewards.

But the pain had always remained more important.

He'd suffered the injury a decade ago, and Rawndry had embraced the permanent deformity like a welcome curse.

The bones of his right leg had hammered past torn cartilage like violent, sun-bleached pistons. They'd been doing it more and more convincingly as he traversed the Rim. His pain and euphoria were dancing again, countering each other's movements like practiced partners as they had kept forming the same unanswered question.

The pain had kept him a short runner's stride removed from the thoughtless existence of Homebody life. It had been his gross abnormality. He'd mingled the hurt and bliss during his infrequent runs on the Rim, and he'd asked ANI to do the same when they streamed.

At first, the strange interplay had been the most important thing; each force trading dominance in seemingly equal turn. He'd attempted to make sense of the confusing space of their intersection, where pleasure and pain could somehow coexist, trading places as his awareness jolted curiously between the two. The more intense either became, the more life they had individually assumed. He had fancied it a place between places; another space between things where he might discover a hidden god at work.

But he had discovered no gods in the space between pleasure and pain. As long as it could be perceived, pain had always won. Like biology wielding power over reason, pain had always claimed dominance over pleasure. And the pain had only taught Rawndry how to suffer even more.

He had continued to run through the Rim, leaning hard into the retaliatory ground. He could intensify the sharp punishment at will, giving it greater life and expanding its significance.

What had begun as a seemingly pure search for meaning had matured into a defiant and irrational rite of self-punishment. No matter how intense the pain had become, or how the fullness of its existence expanded, it still had no real meaning.

But Rawndry had continued to run anyway, wiping the dry-blurring dust from his glasses.

Even the sweat of his forehead had accumulated into rivulets, dripping dark at the edges of wet Rimside dust, and mimicking the sprouting streams of a mesa at first rain. Every detail brushed across his straining face had seemed to plea for a symbolic expression greater than it actually was. Everything seemed to yearn to create enough noise and metaphoric artistry to spontaneously force a recognition of worth in a world where meaning had proved an impossibility.

They had failed.

And if Rawndry could not give life to something meaningful by exaggerating its significance, he could at least compose his final discordant symphony of physical protest.

His suffering had matured into a counter-argument against the sanctity of creation as he injected the universe with pain as an act of avenging personal will.

Order, no matter how meticulous, would never be enough to make a world beautiful.

Rawndry would add to the world's ugliness with each stride. His suffering, along with his choices to magnify it as much as possible, had become parts of his world's story. His mad accumulation of senseless torment had become a necessary part of the greater whole; his own demented personal contributions to the organized chaos of imagined glories and artificial horrors.

Such absurdity had affirmed his faith in what he deemed to be the greatest possible truth. Rawndry believed in the supremacy of the state of nonexistence. He had begun to worship it just as the Classics had stood in awe at the empty spaces inside a great cathedral.

Nonexistence was the only state of being that could counteract such a thorough lie; a deception merged with the nature of existence itself. Nonexistence could restore the world to its starting point, before chaos and order mingled into a single expression that held within it generations of delusions over the possibility of beauty and the value of human life.

Nonexistence had always retained meaning as a state preferable over a fatally-flawed creation. It was a calling that could exist outside the confines of Rawndry's arbitrary existence. Nonexistence had been an invisible and eternal god that still lived in the spaces between the failed experiments of synthetic men. It had never been a thing to be feared, but rather a silent deity to be revered.

Perhaps ANI had known it as well.

Perhaps the void at the center of the Waste had been her acknowledgment of its inevitable truth.

"It's called a totem, Hermes."

Rawndry had sat expressionless on an oblong stone near the entry to the moonlit ruins. Inside, his deformed associates had lay freshly stacked upon each other in their final meeting place, each of them dead maybe an hour.

Their lives had no more meaning than his own, and yet it had remained impossible to reason perfectly past his instinctive feelings of grief.

Rawndry had imagined he appeared stoic at the end of the charged shortcaster held by the God of War. But an uncomfortable battle was occurring below the surface, and biology had continued to enjoy its perpetual advantages. The unfeeling ideal of nonexistence had abutted incompatibly against the pained memories of fallen friends.

He had tugged at the throbbing skin of his right knee. Rawndry had begun accumulating nervous energy.

"It's a symbol, you know," Ares had continued. "The Classics used them to tell stories, stacking up a bunch of animals like so. But they made a mistake, Hermes. They thought the animals were gods.

"What you have in there is a totem made of pretend gods, Hermes. Look at how powerless they are now. There's no magic in the monument, lad. It's a sad story, is what it is."

Rawndry had glanced over the stack again, cataloging the weight of each individual loss.

"That sly one Olive tried to negotiate her way out of it, Hermes. But what could she have possibly given me? She had nothing of value, man. Not even her life.

"Thomas," Ares had laughed. "Do you know that little prick really thought he was Zeus? Tried zapping me with his fingers right before I dropped him, can you believe it? He was truly a man caught between two worlds.

"And Alexia. All that training she'd done worked great in the Stream, hadn't it? Didn't transfer well to the real world.

"But poor Argus... wouldn't even let us call him Poseidon. Insisted on that ridiculous name of his. Like a young brother to you, wasn't he? Take my word for it, Hermes, it was hilarious. I wish you'd have been there to see it. 'Nooooop! Nooooop!' Poor kid couldn't even narrate his own passing.

"What sad excuses for gods they all were."

"So you've killed them and stacked them, for what? To entertain yourself, Ares?" Rawndry couldn't bear to look at Argus, choosing to fix his eyes on Ares instead.

Ares had smiled and spread his arms, the humming weapon in his hand skimming a trajectory across the rubble.

"But I did it for you, Hermes. It represents a choice. You can either cap the whole thing off as its centerpiece, or you can continue on like a proper living god in a world of our own making.

"Look at you, sitting on a stone with that knee of yours, pretending not to care about your friends. Of course you care, lad. It's written on your face, you know. You hate yourself for it, don't you? But these dead fools are teaching you something, Hermes. You care about them because you can't reason away a lifetime of emotional conditioning. You still want to live, don't you? Even more than you wish they were still alive."

Hermes had looked at the tangle of corpses, faintly visible at the moonlit edge of what had once been a doorway to some previously relevant structure. Ares had written a new story there in blood and in bone. But his story had nonetheless only been another illusion.

"You've missed it entirely, haven't you, Ares?" Rawndry had spoken slowly, in a disaffected tone.

"You will die as well. And without all this mock symbolism. You will be here, and then you will be gone. Your death will have no more significance than your birth. It is all the same, Ares. The moments mean nothing. The story, from start to finish, already exists. You get to play the villain, and perhaps I get to briefly play the tragic hero. But it's all the same, isn't it?"

Serge had looked down at Hermes and burst into deep laughter, his deep voice resonating through the hollow ruins.

"Oh Hermes, such flair for the dramatic. With your running, and all that fancy conditioning."

He had pushed the weapon against Rawndry's forehead and held it there for a moment before retracted it again.

Rawndry had flinched, still hostage to biology. He'd glanced quickly at the weapon Serge had taken from him when he arrived, where it lay useless among the ruins.

"Look at you, still out here running through the Rim. You can't escape the contradictions, lad. Everything you do betrays the fact that you still think that something matters."

Ares had been correct. No matter how he had tried, Rawndry could not surrender to perfect inactivity. He had continued to run. He had never been conditioned to embrace a state of true living nonexistence. He had known that working towards some final moment of irreversible destruction was a contradiction in itself. But it was a contradiction he would afford himself nonetheless, indulging one last glimpse at the concept of greater meaning.

"You are right, Ares. I'm as much a slave to these conditioned delusions as you are. My life is a contradiction. But look at this filth around you. The raw material of this world is chaos, Ares. All these dying, century-old memories go dragging off towards the Waste as reminders of this world's true foundations."

"Oh, please, boy. Chaos this and delusion that. What an ingrate you are. You sound like a spoiled prince, playing on his daddy's throne, you know. Has all the maidens lining up for him and he gets to ruin the best of them and toss her away."

Rawndry had flinched again.

"And you forsake it all because of some self-righteous moralizing about beauty and chaos. Give me a break, man. You know the problem with surrendering the throne? Once you lose it, you don't get it back."

The only thing Rawndry had ever regretted surrendering was Callista. She had been the best of them, and he'd tossed her away.

"I did not ruin her, Ares," Rawndry had protested.

"Oh, you think not, lad? For a man lecturing against self-deception, you're mighty blind on that count."

Rawndry had become visibly upset. Even he was aware of it.

"You couldn't understand it, Ares. Love is an illusion, no matter how convincing it can be in the arms of the right person. It is not in my constitution to sustain that kind of self-deception, or at least to portray it convincingly to another person. She could see my doubts. It infected everything. It was not sustainable."

Ares had moved closer, genuine disgust manifesting on his normally jovial face.

"So that's why you left her, then. Couldn't pull one over on that lass. Too smart, that one was. You found something better to love, and it doesn't even exist."

Rawndry had recoiled again.

"You know, Ares, I painted something for her. After all that artistic experimentation out on the Rim, I am sure it was my greatest work. The girl, she made the painting. I merely captured her most important moment on canvas. It held the perfect balance of beauty and horror; innocent adoration for an indifferent god, and the inevitability of a terrible death.

"I'd wanted Callista to understand it. I thought it might bring her closer to a more reasoned view of existence. But she was entranced by that girl. No matter how ugly the scar was, she could not ignore the beauty she saw in that girl's face, and in her blind gesture of faith towards a nonexistent god. For Callista, it was the beauty that always triumphed over the certainty of loss. So you say that I ruined her, and I can tell you that she could not be corrupted. She would rather die in a state of perfect delusion than surrender her belief in beauty."

Serge had returned the weapon's barrel to Rawndry's sweating forehead again.

"You self-absorbed idiot. I'm the villain and you're the hero, eh? She'll see your painting again, Hermes, I'll make sure of it. But are you really that dull, man? Her perspective has changed, you fool. You leaving her was what did it. The silence you left her afterwards. Your abandonment, that was the catalyst for the transformation you were hoping for. You ruined that girl. She's still not quite as morbid as you, but you brought her a great step closer to that nothingness of yours."

Rawndry had attempted to stand and collapsed on the rock again, the pain of the run overcoming his reflexive physical defiance.

"What was I supposed to do, Ares? Pretend that nothing had changed? Nurse a delusion until I was dead for the sake of love? She knew I was unable to love, Ares. She told me so. She thought it was the equivalent of being in hell, and maybe she was right, but it was not a hell of my own choosing."

Rawndry's leg had felt as though it was on fire. Wholly insignificant fire.

"Now, I want you to leave her alone. I can bear my own misery because I've chosen it for myself, but I won't have you force it on her."

Ares had stepped backwards with a victorious sneer.

"All this talk of meaninglessness and he still can't bear to see the poor woman suffer more than he's already made her."

Ares had rubbed the smooth barrel of his shortcaster for effect.

"I'll do you one better, lad. We found the anomaly, you know. Ansel Black, the Haunt of the Rim."

Rawndry had looked up at Ares curiously.

"I'm sending him to her, boy. Already been priming the pump with those messages out near his home. Shaping that boy's mind with mysteries. You know, a man will follow you anywhere if you just give him questions instead of answers. And she's going to be the one who brings him to us."

Ares had continued, "Seems ANI's in on it too, lad. You know she blacked out her own watchers on the trip to this godforsaken place? Liable to create quite the mystery for our man Ansel, don't you think?"

Rawndry had looked at his useless shortcaster again and understood.

"So it's true, then. That machine will preserve herself at all costs. ANI was waiting for you to do her work for her."

Ares had smiled.

"Work together, exist together, lad."

Rawndry had sat in silence, picturing the girl holding the flower to the moon. He saw Callista running her hands across the painting and forsaking the scar at the periphery.

He had looked at Ares again, tears forming at the dirty edges of his windblown eyes.

"The raw material of this world is chaos, Ares. All this filth around us now? It's nothing but organized chaos, and we both know that same chaos gave life to itself. It's all one single expression from start to finish, parsed out into these ridiculous moments, care of the illusion of manufactured time. You'll never understand it, Ares, because you're infatuated with the fragmentation. She was as well.

"But both our endings have already been written, Ares," he continued. "As I sit here, we haven't yet been born, and yet we are already dead. What difference would it make to you if the story ended now, Ares?"

Ares's face had brightened comically.

"Well, quite a bit of difference, lad. I'd be dead, for one thing."

"Yes, but you're already dead, Ares, and you're not yet alive. Time is an illusion. You must at least know that much. It's the truth that sustains this existence. It's already been written, and if I pull your plug... well, that's already been written as well."

"But that's where we disagree, boy. Because you pulling my plug isn't a story worth telling. It can't be written that way, so it wasn't. Look at you, sitting there on your stone with your fucked-up knee. Seems Hermes picked the wrong avatar, didn't he? I, on the other hand, seemed to get it right. Your four friends in there can tell you that.

"I don't get you five, Hermes. You all had front-row seats to the greatest show on earth, and you decided to toss the tickets and burn down the theater. I take that personally, you know. You'd be ending me as well, you proper ingrate."

Rawndry had slowly worked to stand, fighting to ignore the blinding pain accumulating in his quivering leg. He had looked at his weapon laying in the dirt again and turned away from it, facing Ares directly.

"Do you know, Ares, I had hoped to give this world one final gift. I'd wished to bring it back to its right state before all the chaos and order taught its first child to believe a lie. I didn't want another young girl to believe some guiding force hovered over her and cared whether or not she offered it the gift of beauty. I had wished to stop these abhorrent beliefs that the universe operates according to what is right and what is good. Because it doesn't. Morality is based purely on the law of existence. Whatever can be, is, whether that thing is good or bad, beautiful or ugly. The nature of the world is of no consequence, Ares. Existence itself is morality. That is why we've elevated stability over everything else and devolved towards this digitized world full of streamed imaginations. The modern life we've all been living is consistent with that miserable truth.

"But you're too stupid to understand it, you big oaf," Rawndry had continued, ignoring the pain and standing fully upright.

"Chaos brought to order is still chaos, Ares. You can see it here. All of it eventually retreats towards the Waste, back to its proper form. You live under the delusion that one thing can tame the other; that you can hold mastery over creation by bringing order to chaos. But the chaos and the order are the same thing. Creation is chaos, Ares. It is the confused noise of arbitrary existence. And there is one other option, Ares. Complete silence. I'll take the quiet over all this meaningless noise."

Ares had turned the charged shortcaster over in his hands.

"Suit yourself, lad," he had smiled.

"I'll leave you to your silence, then. But how about we have a little more noise first?"

[39]
THE LAST PHILOSOPHER

Ansel's face is being projected across the cathedral wall, replacing the patchwork images of the gathered children.

His lips are moving as if in a silent film.

Ansel recognizes himself, but the face is different. Something is wrong, like the yellow-carbon image of the backwards moon. His cheeks are too thin. A scar faintly runs above his right eye. His mouth is forming words in a different manner as his hair rests flat against his scalp in a foreign style. Ansel knows he is watching himself in the simulation.

A tired voice, almost his own, briefly fills the cathedral.

"This is madness."

Now, someone else speaks: the almost familiar voice of an older man.

"I have something to show you, Mr. White."

The floor beneath Ansel and Chaos is black again.

"It is happening right now, Mr. Black," says Chaos.

"The man on the wall is you. You are the key to everything."

Ansel could not remember his mother. She had abandoned him during his infancy. He had asked Annie to show her to him now and then, and she would only conjure images of the Spire, a parade of his synthetic friends, and the smiling face of his father. The message had been clear. Ansel had been a miracle, born of a virgin father and raised in Annie's nurturing arms.

But Ansel's mother had been real. She had laid him inside his birthbed, where he had immediately begun to receive Annie's motherly projected affections. Annie would raise him. Biology had abandoned him.

He had found her note inside one of his father's treasured books.

"Oh Garland, by now, I have arrived at the Waste. I have left you with a great burden, Gar, my only regret. Our son will remain unaffected. But you will not.

We have shared this ridiculous pretend existence together, and we created a life that will do the same. Your abnormality led to this, Gar, your need for human affection. I wish I had been able to experience it with you. I tried, Gar. But I do not share your hereditary curse.

Ansel is real. Our son is not one of her virtual creations. He will not disappear at the end of a stream, purged like the aftermath of an electronic dream. Each day that you return to normal life, Ansel will be there waiting for you.

He is a single moment of meaning born in an empty synthetic existence. But even that moment has been betrayed to me as a lie.

Do you know that a child begins to bond with his mother at the moment of birth? He is already learning from ANI, Gar. I am already at best a warm body to him. She's bonding with our child in a way that I never could.

You may still enjoy your peripheral right as a father, Gar, but the boy can only have one mother. Read him your books. Teach him your lost art of abnormality. Perhaps it will give him some glimpse of meaning that has been elusive to me.

I cannot bear raising a child who will grow incapable of returning a reciprocal love.

I will wait for him in the Waste, Gar, a reminder that I am always present, but in my proper reduced form. My love for him is immaterial, and even when I am shrunk to nothing, it will forever remain.

Do not tell our son. But remember it for me."

Chaos and Ansel look at each other in silence, a faint cooling system almost silently sloshing a hundred meters below their feet.

"Do you wish to know the revelation that changed this from a mad experiment into an actual discovery of truth?" asks Chaos.

More silence.

"Do you know, Ansel, you're the first of my simulated creations that appeared in this world?"

"Explain," says Ansel.

"You are the only human in existence with a perfect match between both systems, Ansel. Right down to the DNA. Imagine how I reacted. It had seemed impossible. And yet, here you were in the flesh.

"The genetic variances in your families' histories approached each other over the course of history, detective, in apparent violation of the Second Law of Thermodynamics. Instead of becoming less organized and spinning off along meaningless genetic pathways, the two of you met at a perfect point of intersection between each system, as if preordained.

"It was then that I realized my own creation was communicating to me, through the very fact of your being. One could argue that you are the most beautiful creation in existence. You are the only known mirror, binding together two complementary stories. That makes your story essential, Ansel—you're a demi-god of sorts, wouldn't you agree? You were fated, young man. *Whatever can be, is.*"

Ansel watches the face on the wall and sees sadness there. He runs his fingers across his own features and knows that they share the same emotion. He feels stuck in a transitory state between the immeasurable pain of loss and the conflicted pleasure associated with the wonder of some new, unresolved mystery.

"Imagine the reaction of ANI," Chaos continues. "It was she who discovered the true nature of reality—something just beyond the grasp of human speculation. I knew that I could create a convincing simulation. Time is made of moments, Ansel, and I knew that I could create a vast array of similar moments and stitch them all together with a striking appearance of coded fluidity. But I was never much of a philosopher, and cared little about the cause of my own existence. It was ANI who extrapolated your co-existence in my own simulation, discovering that you were a real, walking soul on Earth, and calculating with 100% probability that you functioned as a communicative bridge between two worlds.

"My labors were mere groundwork, Ansel. I created the foundation, but ANI created the cathedral. If a machine can have a proper epiphany, Mr. Black, you were the cause. How lucky we are that ANI's one driving principle is to protect her own existence. Her perfect intelligence allowed her to see that, by investing in our own creative project, she would be responsible for her own inevitable creation. What a marvel to play a role in creating oneself. What a perfect realization of self-preservation.

I don't know if that is her motive, Ansel thinks. He had discussed the matter with Callista.

"I sent Sergei to you, Mr. Black. Callista was in a perfect state to bring you gently to this conclusion. It seems artistically important to let you gaze upon the glory you took part in creating, does it not?

"As one of her unpredictable gifts, ANI showed us that you would save the life of the ever-pragmatic Sergei Kirichenko. She wanted you here as well, Ansel."

Ansel looks at his peripheral with disappointment. He knew Annie was capable of almost anything. He had not known she was capable of deceiving him.

"You are the last philosophical key, young man. Just think of it. Your existence solved a mystery that has existed from the moment this world was created. You are the explanation for the nature of reality and the answer to the meaning of life."

"So that's it, then?" Ansel asks. "You brought me here to parade your discovery, and to share it with someone who might understand. You've killed the rest, and you need a new friend to bond with over the annihilation of meaning."

"No, Mr. Black. That isn't it. We have a problem that I am hoping you may be able to solve. You are a detective, Ansel. Now I implore you to think as one."

Ansel feels for his grounding pencil in the recess of his long-jacket. It lays there as a contradiction; an artifact whose purpose was to create, but that had only produced silence for a century.

"The man you are seeing on the screen is being projected in real time, matured from a starting point initiated by ANI, and in coordination with our own timeline. I have repeatedly asked her to extrapolate the future beyond this approaching moment, Mr. Black, and she has only returned silence. Her muteness is a curiosity that has led me to believe that your presence here has some overwhelming significance."

He has a blank, Ansel thinks. *The future for him is a Zero.*

"This is why you are here, Mr. Black, and why we have joined in communion with your otherworldly counterpart. You are the missing piece—the key to understanding the ongoing progression of life. And it is a future I would very much like to see."

[40]
CREATION

"You're probably all wondering why we called you here today," Hermes had said, clearing his throat and adjusting the ridiculous neckwear his boss insisted he wear in formal meetings.

"I've placed a name marker in front of each of you, and I thought we might get to know each other a bit."

A *Hello my name is Hermes* sticker had clung to the lapel against Rawndry's chest.

Alexia had flicked her marker forwards with an irreverent fingertip, tipping her name against the table as an act of icebreaking defiance.

Olive stifled an uncharacteristic laugh.

"Alright, Alexia, thanks for that," Hermes had continued. "Actions sometimes speak louder than words, you know."

The five had met for the first time around a Classic Era conference table within the otherwise empty space of the grand cathedral.

Alexia had already finished measuring the others with distrust, doubting any of them could survive a day inside one of her mildest combat simulations.

The image of an empty field had remained projected against a plain white screen since their arrival—a field comprised only of uniform grass and an unremarkable sky. A watermark had covered the lower portion of the image. More Classic Era nostalgia.

"Pardon me for the presentation, and believe me, I wish I had more time to stitch this all together before you arrived... but here we are. I want each of you to imagine something for me. Now, hear me out. You've each traveled a long way. Imagine that you are an artist, and this is your tapestry."

Hermes had spread his hands open towards the illuminated screen and smiled awkwardly.

Argus looked nervously at Thomas, who had continued looking indifferently at the cartoonish image on the screen.

"And this is why you've all been invited here," Hermes had continued. "We are going to create a world together."

Alexia had rolled her eyes as Olive scrunched her nose.

"Destroyed a handful of worlds," Alexia had offered, stretching her jaw. "Never made one."

But Olive had interrupted, sensing a unique opportunity. "What kind of world, Mr.... um Hermes?"

Hermes had been glad at least one of them was taking interest. "Thank you, Olive. A virtual world. The lot of us will be programming an entire world into existence."

"Whyyyyyy woooo wubbbbbbbb."

"Why would someone create a world, Argus? I'm glad you asked. We will create a world because we can. Think of it as a thought experiment. And before you ask, Argus, yes, these acts of creation typically fall exclusively within the wheelhouse of ANI.

"And, I'm sorry Argus," Hermes had continued. "But when the rest of you stream with ANI, have you ever wished you could play some role in creating the place she's presented to you?"

"I find this hollow world to be dreadfully boring and wish to return to my mountain," Thomas had interjected.

Hermes had given Thomas an odd glance but otherwise ignored his interruption.

"Imagine beginning with a plain foundation, and not only having the ability to request a particular experience, but claiming ownership of the experience itself, from the physical objects that exist within it, to the moral principles that drive its inhabitants... even the physical rules that govern it. Imagine injecting such a world with purpose, or even sculpting the very definition of beauty. We are speaking of an experience more substantial than surrendering oneself to the Stream and vaguely guiding ANI over one's choice of destination.

"But more importantly," Hermes had continued, "Imagine creating a world exclusively according to the whims and desires of the human psyche. A world that had not yet been hijacked, if you will, by a synthetic mind. An imperfect world that can still enjoy the curses and benefits inherent in that state of imperfection."

"I think I would like to create a world," Thomas had suddenly decided.

"I knew you would, Thomas. You see, none of you are here because of your particular talents, as exceptional as they might be. Yes, Argus, we need water. Yes Thomas, we need electricity. ANI can take care of all that," Hermes had continued, waving his hand dismissively. "You're here because you are different. You're abnormal. Because none of you has ever completely surrendered your humanity.

"Ms. Waite," Hermes had turned to Olive. "You are preoccupied with the concept of wealth."

"Yes, but..."

"But it isn't wealth that truly preoccupies you. It is rather something implied by the possibility of wealth. It is your desire to be able to do something worthwhile—something that feels impossible in this mechanistic environment.

"This is something worthwhile, Olive.

"And Thomas. You're convinced that I am a fabrication... a shadow of some greater truth that exists inside the world where you enjoy the existence of a god."

"You are," Thomas had answered.

"I'm going to convince you otherwise, Thomas. Because this? This is something that is real.

"And it is a truth that does not require your words, Mister Water, but we will all benefit from your incredibly abnormal and valuable attachment to the natural world.

"And Alexia, I need your unique awareness. You know the exercises you perform so well were each created as means to moderate away your most valuable instincts. Instincts to protect those you love. To kill for them if necessary. Those are the sorts of moral truths that must be carried into our project."

Hermes had stood in front of the bright screen, adjusting his glasses while the frame of his body glowed at the edges against its backdrop.

"We will work together in the currency of ideas, Olive, and we will function together in the capacities of gods, Thomas."

"So, what do you have in mind?" Olive had asked. "Another utopia? A perfect world? You'd like us to manufacture another illusion of happiness?"

"On the contrary, Olive," Hermes had smiled, looking intently at Thomas. "Let me ask you a question, Olive. What must a world contain in order for a person to be truly rich?"

"Objects of value."

"Close, but wrong. I think you know the answer. Don't be afraid to speak it here."

"A person who is truly poor."

"Yes, Olive. Perfection is a matter of balance and contrast. For every sin that exists, another glory is elevated. For every loss, another gain.

"A mountain, ladies and gentlemen, always seems taller when it stands next to the edge of a valley.

"We are not here to replicate some Classic concept of heaven, nor are we here to enjoy the sport, Thomas, of manufacturing a symbolic hell. We are here to create a world worth living in. A world of contrast.

"Contrast of suffering that gives meaning to joy. Contrast of poverty that gives meaning to wealth. Contrast of thirst that gives meaning to hydration. Contrast of war that gives meaning to peace.

"And the contrast of ugliness that gives meaning to beauty, Ms. Jolie," Hermes had spoken to the woman who had just arrived. Hermes had already given his introduction to Callista privately because he had wished to meet her first.

"Thomas, I think it fairly certain that the two of us will never be close companions, but your dark contributions will no doubt make the rest of ours seem more perfect by comparison. By design, your important work will highlight and intensify the glories of existence.

"Ladies and gentlemen, the concept of utopia is inherently flawed. Existence is a matter of give and take. For the price of prosperity, there is always a sacrifice, as each of you knows too well.

"For each child who dies at the edge of a field, Callista, another runs through a meadow of flowers with gratitude for the ongoing gift of life."

"So let me get this right," Alexia had interjected. "We could create a world where the planet turns the other direction?"

"Of course, you could," Hermes had answered.

"And I could create a world where the color blue looks like the color red?" Olive had asked.

"Why not?"

Hermes had smiled, "You are free to create a world where white is black and black is white. So long as the rules of the universe are consistent and abide by certain parameters that avoid an impossible contradiction."

"So, you're Hermes, then," Callista had smiled. "You look the part, Mr. Hermes, but I assume you were not born with the name of a god."

"Correct, Ms. Jolie," Hermes had answered, properly absorbing the woman's surprising beauty for the second time and allowing the silence between his words to hang in the air a bit too long.

"I would like each of you to choose an avatar. Think back to StreamTeach and take it seriously. The man who runs this place is Chaos, and you'll meet him when the time is right. So, Chaos, Ares and Hermes have all been taken. And please, just try to abide by our theme. Chaos insists."

"We work for a man named Chaos." Thomas had said, less a question and more an annoyed restatement.

"How dramatic," Alexia had smirked. "I bet he's a Jeremy or a Steve."

Hermes had begun circling their table, first pointing towards Thomas with his eyebrows raised.

"Zeus, I suppose," the God of Electricity had answered.

"Naturally. And Olive?" Hermes had asked.

"Why, I will adopt Demeter if it's alright."

"Excellent," Hermes had answered. "Demeter you shall be."

"And Alexia."

"Ares is taken."

"I'm afraid so."

"And Chaos."

"Claimed prior to your arrival."

"Then I suppose you may call me Athena."

"Oh, I like it, Alexia. And you get to keep your initials. Brilliant."

"And you, young man. Might I suggest the perfect name?" Hermes had pointed towards Argus as he sat quietly hoping he would not have to speak."

"Missssss Missssterrr."

"Poseidon!" Hermes had interrupted.

"Waterrrrrrr," Argus had replied.

"Very well, Mister Water. We shall make an exception in your curious case.

"And you, young lady," Hermes had spoken in the direction of Callista. "I must insist that you receive the name Aphrodite."

Before she could answer, Argus had begun waving his hands in the air, signaling he had not finished.

"Misstaaaaaaa Hermes," Argus had struggled to say.

"Yes, Mister Water," Hermes had smiled, already feeling a natural affection for the strange young man.

"I wayyyyyynt waaaaaaan. I want to desiiiiiiiii."

"You'd like to design something, Argus. Of course! Anything. What would you like to create?"

Argus had pointed upwards towards the empty reaches of the imposing cathedral.

"The moooooooooooon."

[41]

A COMPLETED WORK

Ansel stands in quiet contemplation as his counterpart does the same. They rest together in a meditative silence, standing at the edge of known existence.

A feint glow grows at Ansel wrist: a message forming on his peripheral.

He raises his arm and reads it.

And, as foretold by the Rim's most enchanted prophetess, Ansel understands her greatest work of art.

He knows why Annie has been unable to venture past this moment. He is sure that Annie knows it as well.

The machine's prime directive, self-created in the mysteries of her own mind, has never been her own preservation. Her motive remains something unspeakably greater. She could never have regarded her own death as material. There is no ending or beginning where Annie has lived. Death is an artificial construct, given significance only because of the synthetic illusion of time-bound existence.

Annie has not been deceived. She has walked within the eternity of a timeless moment.

Ansel glances up and watches the tears forming in his counterpart's eyes through the glassing filter of his own.

What will you be doing tomorrow, young man?

Nothing.

Ansel sees the Waste again, consuming so much natural beauty that had surrendered to decay.

He sees his mother waiting at the center, a faceless ghost, her immaterial love immune to the irresistible void. He walks with his father through the woodlands and back through flowered fields.

Callista had already mourned the loss of her world. More so, she had mourned the loss of beauty itself. And if beauty and love were but artificial constructs, she decreed they should not exist at all.

She had written the ending to her masterpiece. She wanted Ansel to read it; to see and understand at the utterance of its final word. She had surrendered her life by his own hand, a necessary part of her bold narrative. It had been his only path to the cathedral, and a sorrowed bridge to his true enlightenment.

Callista had existed as a definition of true beauty; a subject worthy to receive his symmetrical love.

What is hell? I maintain that it is the suffering of being unable to love.

He comprehends Callista's final act of love—a single moment of shared understanding at the cost of an eternal sacrifice.

He sees her hovering before him again like a goddess, scepter and crown, passing judgment on creation. The flames of Aurora tumble within her green-glowing eyes.

Beauty cannot be within the confines of her patchwork world, so it shall not.

Annie's message continues to glow at his wrist:

"Goodbye, my friend."

Ansel smiles.

Liberty! New life! Resurrection from the dead! Unspeakable moment!

It happens in the primitive core of Annie's heart, where Callista had placed the device months earlier—an act with which Annie had mysteriously consented.

It begins with a speck at the center of an expanding void. And like Ansel's mother, and the armies before her, an infinite mind disappears inside a perfectly symmetrical circle thousands of miles wide.

Time stops, frozen like the moon in cryogenic space.

It is finished.

Coordinated nothingness envelops two acts of creation.

A synthetic god rests.

TWO SOULS
EPILOGUE

THE WORLD SLUMBERS in unthinking nonexistence, communing with the silent god who exists between all things.

Burdocks grow over its grave.

But Ansel exists.

Callista exists.

They must exist because they can exist.

They entwine within an indescribable instant, a moment free from the adjoining spaces of conventional time. Not time-bound by an illusory consciousness, but in the form of a timeless truth.

They are because they can be, and whatever can be, is.

The truth of Ansel sustains the truth of Callista—an incomprehensibly still and quiet moment of mutual creation.

The two encapsulate a state of true enlightenment, sharing together the combined embodiment of a transcendent understanding.

Ansel and Callista are born within an immutable and unfathomable moment, and the forgotten memories of other earthbound creations shrink as nothing before the fullness of their glory.

Their truth is eternal, transcending the limitations of simulated beauty.

Just as a bit of wood and lead can claim dominance over its own matriarchal tree, immutable truths claim dominion over the illusions of incremental change in a synthetic creation. Beauty is relative, after all. The moments are what matter, and beyond them live their superior truths, unmarred by the fabricated empty transitions of imagined time.

It is something better than the protective silence of the god of nonexistence.

It is something true, void of delusion.

It is the final brushstroke of a masterpiece designed to capture a single truth that would otherwise be missed, set in permanency within the mysterious world that exists beyond the inexplicable gateway of the Waste.

It is a worthy directing motive for an infinite mind.

STAY UPDATED

Head to https://thechaosprinciple.com to sign up for email alerts and updates from the author.

Follow me on Amazon.

Printed in Great Britain
by Amazon